MURDER IS A HATE CRIME

A HANNAH KLINE MYSTERY

PAULA BERNSTEIN

M&Z PRESS

In memory of Dr. Wayne Dodge,
beloved brother-in-law and extraordinary physician.

CHAPTER ONE

D ETECTIVE BRENDA JORDAN'S CELL PHONE RANG AT 5:45 a.m. Her girlfriend, Marcy, groaned, rolled over and put a pillow over her head.

"Jordan here. Hold on," Brenda said. She tiptoed out of bed and took the phone into the bathroom, so she could talk without further disturbing Marcy, who was not a morning person. Brenda was not supposed to be on call until 7:00 a.m.

"What's going on?"

"Dead body, probable homicide at Pico and Sepulveda, under the freeway," the dispatcher said. "Detective Rodriguez has his hands full with a home invasion in Bel Air and asked if you'd take it."

Brenda rolled her eyes. No detective liked to catch a murder case an hour before going off duty, but Rodriguez was a good guy and rarely took advantage of his fellow detectives. If he'd said he was tied up, it was probably the truth.

"I'll be there in twenty minutes," Brenda said.

She'd taken the precaution of leaving her morning

clothes in the bathroom the previous night, so she wouldn't wake Marcy when she dressed. Marcy worked for a Santa Monica architectural firm, and her work day began at nine.

Pulling on pants, a turtleneck and a jacket, Brenda washed her face, brushed her teeth and ran a comb through her blonde bob. As she left the bathroom and closed the bedroom door behind her, she noticed that Marcy had fallen asleep again. Removing her gun and shoulder holster from the safe in her hall closet, Brenda grabbed her keys and headed for her car. It wouldn't take more than ten minutes to drive from her Culver City apartment to the homeless camp.

When she arrived, she was pleased to see that the officers who found the body had already installed crime scene tape and were keeping onlookers away. She didn't recognize either of the patrolmen, and assumed they were among the new batch of cadets who had recently graduated. She exited her car and pulled out her badge.

"Detective Brenda Jordan. What's the story?"

The tall, round-faced cop with neatly cut black hair, introduced himself. "Alberto Figueroa, ma'am. We found the homeless camp deserted except for one dead body. His head is bloody, so I'm assuming homicide."

Brenda pulled on a pair of paper shoe covers and latex gloves, and slipped under the tape. "Have you called the evidence team and the coroner yet?" she asked.

"No, ma'am."

Brenda wasn't quite used to *ma'am*. It made her feel elderly, but compared to those two twenty-year-olds, thirty-five was probably ancient.

"Go ahead and call them. I'm going to take a look." She glanced around the homeless encampment. "Where is everyone?"

"They probably cleared out to avoid talking to the police."

"They'll be back tonight. It's supposed to rain again," Brenda said.

Brenda swept the ground with her flashlight, walking carefully so as not to step on anything that looked as if it could be evidence. The victim appeared to be a middle-aged black man. Curly hair, with a receding hairline, was slicked back with gel. He had a full beard, which was well-groomed, and she could see clotted blood on the pavement under his head.

Grasping the blanket with two gloved fingers, she folded it back to inspect his clothes and to search for a wallet. He was wearing jeans and a worn, black leather jacket. The pockets she could reach were empty. Brenda unzipped the jacket, revealing a white T-shirt. There was no sign of blood. He hadn't been stabbed or shot, at least not from the front. She'd wait until the medical examiner arrived and turned him over to check his back.

Wondering if he'd been beaten, she raised the T-shirt, looking for bruising. What she found instead were two flattened breasts.

Brenda quickly replaced the jacket and blanket, not wanting to interfere with the body's temperature.

"This may be a hate crime," she announced. "This guy is trans."

CHAPTER TWO

DR. HANNAH KLINE, DRESSED IN SCRUBS AND IN A hurry, flipped the switch on her coffee maker, taking a deep breath as the tantalizing scent of Arabia Mocha Java perfused the kitchen.

"Can I try some, Mommy?" Zoe, Hannah's seven-year-old daughter was working her way through a bowl of Cheerios.

Hannah tried to remember how old she was when she first asked to try the magic grownup beverage. Surely not seven.

"Coffee and wine are grownup drinks. You probably won't like the taste." All Zoe needed was caffeine and more energy. As it was, Hannah wished she could bottle some of her child's endless physical stamina and drink it before going to the office. "When you're a little older, I'll mix some with your milk," she promised.

She poured herself a mug, took an English muffin out of the toaster, buttered it, added some marmalade, and finally sat down for a minute. Daniel, her husband, dressed for his job as a senior detective at the LAPD, walked into the kitchen.

"There's coffee," she said, nodding toward the counter. Ordinarily she'd have poured some for him too, but she was demonstrating her displeasure.

Spring break was beginning next weekend, and Josh, Daniel's recently discovered son, was supposed to arrive on Saturday from Washington State to spend it with them. They had agreed, months ago, that it would be Daniel's responsibility to break the news to Zoe that she had an older stepbrother. How he was going to explain his youthful affair to a seven-year-old was his problem. Hannah had no plan to get involved.

"I have an early surgery this morning," she said. "I'll drop Zoe off at her carpool on my way to Memorial."

Daniel poured some coffee into his car thermos and stuffed a granola bar into his shirt pocket. "Brenda just called. I have to meet her and the team at a scene."

"Zoe, sweetie, go get your backpack and your rain jacket. We're leaving in a few minutes."

As soon as Zoe left the kitchen, Hannah turned to Daniel. "At the risk of nagging, Zoe is going to need some time to get used to the idea of a brother. You need to tell her tonight after dinner."

"Honestly, I haven't been procrastinating. We only signed the financial agreement last week, so I wasn't sure I'd get the time with Josh I requested. He's really excited about coming to LA and meeting Zoe. I promise I'll tell her today."

Hannah relented and gave him a smile. "Josh seems like a nice kid. I took the week off. I hope your latest murder case isn't going to interfere with our family time."

"Brenda's a very competent detective. I'm sure she can

handle anything that we don't finish this week. Gotta run." He bent over, kissed her lips, and headed out the door.

CHAPTER THREE

BRENDA HEARD A PEAL OF LAUGHTER. SPINNING around she saw that Alberto Rodriguez had been peering over her shoulder at the murder victim.

"It's not funny," she snarled.

"Sorry, ma'am. I've just never seen a guy with a beard and boobs before."

"Do you have any idea how many black trans people are murdered every year in hate crimes?"

Alberto shook his head. "They talked a little about hate crimes at the Academy, but mostly based on race or religion."

Brenda calmed herself. This was a moment for education, not anger.

"People who are LGBT, and especially trans, are frequently victims of hate. Almost half of trans people have been sexually assaulted during their lives, and something like ten percent have been physically attacked. Of the murder victims, the majority have been black trans women, although Latinas have also been murdered."

"I knew there were trans women," Alberto said. "I never gave a thought to a woman becoming a man."

"There are probably as many trans men as there are women," Brenda said, "and if you ask them, they don't think of it as becoming a man. They've always been a man, just stuck in the wrong body."

She watched Alberto's face as he processed this information. It was a thoughtful face, not one that suggested homophobia. The other rookie was also listening, although she couldn't see his expression.

"You know quite a bit about this," Alberto said.

Brenda shrugged. "Before I was assigned to the West LA station, I worked West Hollywood. I got to know quite a few trans people." She'd also connected to the LGBT community for the first time, and had begun to face her own feelings, but that wasn't anything she'd ever share with anyone at work.

A moment later the Coroner's van pulled up, followed shortly by Daniel's Mustang. Dr. Bill Pincus, Brenda's favorite medical examiner, exited the van. Brenda briefed both of them, and she and Daniel stepped back to let Bill examine the body.

Bill took a temperature, checked for rigor mortis, and turned the body over looking for lividity.

"What time was he found?" Bill asked.

"Five-thirty," Alberto answered.

"And you're sure he was dead when you found him?"

"My partner checked his pulse."

"So, time of death?" Daniel asked.

"Anywhere between one-and-a-half and two hours ago. There's no rigor mortis, his temperature's ninety-six and there's very little lividity. I'd say someone whacked him on the back of his head, fractured his skull, lacerated his scalp and left him to die. The only question is whether they attacked him here or brought him here, and dumped him while he was still alive. I'd like to complete the autopsy before weighing in on that."

Daniel turned to Brenda. "Do you think the residents of the encampment heard this happen and split, or found him dead and ran before the police came?"

"Either way, they'll be back. They left their tents and all their stuff. We should get a few plain clothes guys to watch the camp after the crime scene team finishes up, and get statements from the residents," Brenda said. "Bill, we don't have an ID on him. Can you expedite collecting finger prints and dental photos? I know you may not get to the autopsy today."

Bill gave her a thumbs up. "Will do."

The photographer and crime scene team were suiting up and getting ready to do their jobs.

"Ready to head to the station?" Daniel asked.

Brenda nodded and they walked silently to their cars.

"Are you okay?" Daniel asked.

Daniel was observant like that. He'd probably sensed her tension.

"No," she said. "I'm angry."

"We'll get the bastards responsible," he said. "I promise."

CHAPTER FOUR

B RENDA TOSSED HER CELL PHONE ONTO HER DESK. "I hate waiting."

"For the fingerprints?" Daniel asked, seating himself at his own desk, next to hers.

"For everything: the fingerprints, which may or may not be in the system, the autopsy results, the trace evidence. I want to start investigating this, and it's hard without an ID."

Every time someone in the LGBT community was attacked, it was as if the hatred, and the crime, were directed personally at her. She had the advantage of being white, and a lesbian who didn't look particularly butch, but that wouldn't protect her if some neo-Nazi spotted her holding hands with, or kissing, Marcy.

"I have a thought," Daniel said. "The victim is obviously on testosterone. How many doctors are there who offer testosterone therapy to trans men? Maybe we get Izzy to Photoshop a picture of him, take out the pool of blood so as not to freak anyone out, and see if one of those doctors might be able to identify him."

Izzy, short for Isadore Washington, was the department's IT specialist.

Brenda shot him a smile. "I knew there was a reason I keep you around," she said. "That's brilliant. We don't even have to wait for the official crime scene photos. I've got some on my phone."

"Why don't you ask Izzy to work with the photo, and I'll start researching physicians?"

"Judging by his clothes, I suspect he either had no insurance or was on MediCal," Brenda said. "Why don't you focus on low cost clinics?"

"Got it," Daniel said, turning to his computer screen.

By the time Brenda emerged from Izzy's office with a stack of sanitized portraits of the victim, Daniel had identified several local clinics that offered hormone therapy to people wishing to transition.

"Our best bets might be Planned Parenthood and the LGBT Center," Daniel said. "They offer specialized services to the trans community. There's also a clinic at UCLA and at Memorial Hospital. Should we split up and divide the work, or be environmentally friendly and take your new car?"

Brenda grinned. "I think my new Chevy Volt will generate a lot less pollution than your vintage Mustang. I know you've been dying to try it out. Would you like to drive?"

"I would."

"Let's start at UCLA and work our way east," Brenda suggested

Daniel adjusted the seat on Brenda's car, and buckled up.

She'd wanted a bright red one, but it was a bit too flashy for undercover work. She showed him how to start it, and gave him a quick tour of the computer screen and its settings.

"Go for it," she said, as he reversed the car out of the parking lot.

~

It was a quick drive to the UCLA hospital building. Daniel left the car with the valet.

"Seriously? Valet parking?" Brenda said.

"It'll save time, and LAPD is paying," Daniel said.

They checked the directory and followed the signs to the Transgender Medicine clinic.

Daniel pulled out his ID and approached the receptionist. "We're detectives Ross and Jordan of the LAPD. Can we see the administrator please?"

"Is something wrong, Detectives?" The receptionist asked.

Brenda couldn't tell if the receptionist was transgender, but she hoped that was the case. A new patient, especially, would need to feel welcomed.

"No. We just need some information."

The receptionist picked up the phone and a few minutes later a short, middle-aged, balding man came out, shook their hands, and escorted them to his office.

"How can I help you?"

"We are trying to identify a Black, transgender man who was found dead this morning with no ID. We're visiting clinics where he may have obtained testosterone, hoping one of the doctors might be able to identify him."

"Doctor Meyers is in this morning. Let me call her."

The doctor was a tall, regal black woman with a gray afro. Her badge said Latisha Meyers, Urology.

Daniel shook hands, handed her a photo, and waited while she examined it.

"I'm sorry. I know all of the regular testosterone patients quite well. I've never seen him."

Brenda felt a flush of disappointment, and something else. Why had she been standing there like an accessory? This was an LGBT murder and it was her case. She'd been first on the scene, even if Daniel was the senior detective in their partnership. She needed to step up and take control.

"I'll drive," she said, as the valet returned her car. "Next stop, Memorial."

Memorial Hospital was where Daniel's wife Hannah practiced. It occupied a substantial campus with research and clinic buildings as well as the main inpatient center. As Brenda drove, Daniel double checked the location of the clinic, and guided Brenda to the parking structure.

This time Brenda stepped up and did the questioning. The result was no different; another dead end.

"Damn it," she said. "I was hoping this would be easier."

"Grunt work is never easy," Daniel said. "We could have assigned a few newbies to do this job. How much trouble could they get into, showing photos to doctors?"

"No trouble, but this situation requires tact and finesse. We haven't had a chance to see if any of the new recruits have any. We can take a few of them with us later when we go to the homeless encampment."

The next stop was the West Hollywood Planned Parenthood, which was another dead end. By this time Brenda was having trouble containing her frustration.

"If the LGBT Center can't help, I don't know what we're going to do next."

"I do," said Daniel. "I'm hungry and there are a bunch of gourmet food trucks in front of the LA County Art Museum. Food is the best medicine. We can hit the LGBT Center after we eat."

Brenda nodded, flooring the accelerator, while keeping her eyes on the Wilshire Boulevard traffic. "I feel agitated," she said, as she blasted past a yellow light. "Hate crimes infuriate me."

"I understand," Daniel said. He was looking a little pale as she navigated back and forth between lanes. "I think you need to take the lead in this case."

"I was thinking the same thing."

"I'll be on vacation next week. Josh is coming to visit, and we're all taking some family time, so if we don't solve this in a few days, you're on your own. I have no doubt you can crack this case without me."

Brenda slowed down.

"I didn't know about Josh. Is Hannah okay with having a new stepson?"

"I think so," Daniel said, "but she wouldn't be okay with my not being there, twenty-four seven."

"Not to worry." She pulled over next to a food truck and got out. "How about buying me a taco?"

In a better mood, and with a full stomach, Brenda drove up to the elegant LGBT center, with its tall columns wrapped in rainbow colors.

"I know the chief administrator well from my stint in Hollywood division. Why don't I do this while you wait? I don't want to intimidate people with two detectives."

That wasn't the only reason she wanted to do this alone. The Center was a special place to her. It was where she felt most comfortable and totally accepted. It was where she'd met Marcy, shortly after she'd left Hollywood division and had returned to the Center to participate in their social events. She knew people. She was at home here, and as much as she cared for Daniel and their friendship, she didn't want to share it.

"Sure," Daniel said. "I don't mind stretching my legs while you detect. Meet you back at the car."

Brenda entered the front door, recognized the receptionist, and asked if Drew Perez, the administrator was available.

"It's nice to see you," the receptionist said. "You haven't been here in awhile."

Moments later she was ushered through the security door into the administrative wing.

"Brenda Jordan, how are you? Are you back in Hollywood?" Drew stood up and reached out to shake Brenda's hand. Drew was tall, thin and had an MBA from UCLA.

"No, I'm a detective at the Westside division, and I'm here because I need your help."

Drew sat back down. "I was afraid this wasn't a social call. What's wrong?"

Brenda briefed him and handed him the photo.

"I don't recognize him, but I don't meet all our patients. Unfortunately Doctor Ryan, who runs our transgender clinic, is only in on Tuesdays and Thursdays. I'll show him this first thing tomorrow."

"Thanks Drew. I seem to be drawing a blank today and if I can't ID this guy, investigating his death will be close to impossible. You know how most transgender murders don't get solved."

"Yeah, I know, but most police departments don't have you. You're one of us, Brenda, and I have complete confidence in you."

Drew's warmth almost brought tears to her eyes, along with a bolt of anxiety. She didn't want to let her community down, but what if she couldn't solve it?

Daniel was waiting for her at the car.

"No dice?" he asked.

"How did you know?"

"I could tell by your face. Maybe the fingerprints will be in the system."

"Maybe. The doctor wasn't in. They'll show him the photo tomorrow. In the meantime, let's get back to the station. I'll recruit some help and see if the occupants of the homeless camp have returned. You can call it a day and get home to Hannah. I'll take care of the paperwork."

"Want me to drive?" Daniel asked, "Or can you get us back without getting arrested for speeding?"

"Point taken," Brenda said as she opened the driver's door.

CHAPTER FIVE

B Y THE TIME BRENDA AND DANIEL REACHED THE Westside station, rain was coming down in sheets and traffic was at a crawl. Brenda pulled up next to Daniel's car so he wouldn't get soaked.

"It never used to rain like this in April," Daniel said.

"Global warming. Go home and dry off," Brenda said.

"Don't work too late. It's been a long day and you'll have more energy tomorrow if you get a nice dinner and a decent night's sleep." Daniel took his car keys out of his pocket and prepared to transfer.

"I won't, but this is the perfect time to find the occupants of the homeless encampment in their tents. I'll take a few guys with me so we can complete the interviews quickly."

Daniel slipped into the driver's seat of his Mustang, wiping his face with the sleeve of his jacket. Brenda waved as he pulled out of the parking lot. She reached for the small umbrella she kept in the side pocket of her car and made a run for the back door of the station.

Two of the newbies were talking in the hallway, and she motioned to them to follow her to her desk. She didn't remember their names, but she thought of them as Tweedledee and Tweedledum because they were hard to tell apart. Both were tall, muscular and sported blonde crew cuts. Their faces were unmemorable except for pale blue eyes.

"I'm Detective Jordan and I need a little help on a case," she said.

The two introduced themselves as Donald McCall and Chuck Henderson. Henderson managed a smile. McCall didn't.

"A man was found murdered this morning in the homeless camp under the freeway on Pico," she said. "We still don't have an ID on him, and the camp was empty this morning. As you might imagine, homeless people don't much like the police. When they see us, they're afraid we're going to clear out the camp. It appears as if someone dumped this man's body here, dead or barely alive after a beating. We need to find out if anyone heard or saw anything last night."

Henderson glanced at his watch. "It's almost end of shift."

"This isn't a nine-to-five job," Brenda said, pissed.

"Do you think any of them will tell us anything?" McCall asked.

"I'm going to come bearing gifts; hot coffee and pastries from the nearest Starbucks. If we're polite and non-threatening, and ask for their help in a respectful manner, we might learn something. We'll take our personal vehicles, not a squad car."

~

With Brenda in the lead, and the men carrying the coffee and pastries, the three of them approached the camp. Once the forensic team had finished, they'd removed the crime scene tape. The tents were unchanged from earlier in the day, and no one was visible. This wasn't surprising. It was dark and chilly, and the wind was blowing rain under the shelter of the freeway.

Brenda stood at the end of the camp, nearest to the crime scene, and called out "Hello, anyone here?"

An elderly woman poked her head out from a nearby tent.

"What you want?"

"My name is Brenda. I've brought a gallon of hot coffee for everyone and some snacks to go with it. What's your name?"

The woman exited her home. She was wearing a black plastic garbage bag, like a poncho, in lieu of a raincoat. Her white hair frizzed in a halo around her wrinkled face and her mouth was missing several teeth.

"Imelda," she said. "Do gooders, huh?"

"It's pretty wet and nasty outside. Is there a place we can put the coffee?"

The woman pointed to a card table, outside another tent and Brenda motioned to the men to set up the drinks. Once she was alone with the woman she said, "I need your help."

"The price for the coffee? What kind of help?"

"I'm a detective and I just need to ask you and the other people living here a few questions. A man's body was found in this camp this morning and we don't know who he is. We were hoping someone might recognize his photo, or might have seen or heard something last night."

"I don't know nothing.'" She turned away.

"Please," Brenda said. "Won't you just look at the picture?" Imelda hesitated and Brenda handed her the flyer.

A relieved expression crossed the woman's face. "Don't know him."

"Did you see or hear anything last night? We think someone dumped his body here and your tent is the closest."

"It's noisy under the freeway. There's traffic above us and next to us. I was asleep and I didn't hear nothing."

"Did you see the body in the morning?"

The woman froze. "Yeah, I saw the blood but I didn't have nothing to do with it."

"I don't think for a minute that you killed him," Brenda said. "I'm trying to find out who did. What time did you find him?"

She shrugged. "Dunno. It was still dark. I hadda pee."

"Did you realize the man was dead?"

"Yeah."

"What did you do then?"

"I woke up the camp and we left before the cops came. They woulda blamed us."

Brenda sighed. "I know you have no reason to trust the police, but honestly, we're just here to see if any of you can help us solve this."

Brenda looked toward the rest of the camp. Several inhabitants were helping themselves to coffee. McCall and Henderson stood back awaiting her orders.

"Thank you Imelda. I appreciate you talking to me."

Brenda wasn't optimistic that any of the other homeless people had heard anything, but she did want to see if the victim could be ID'd. Joining the two rookies, she shared the flyers and instructed them to begin asking questions. She was interested in seeing how they handled the job.

~

They both approached the men who were helping themselves to pastries and tried to talk to them individually.

"Would you mind if I asked you a question?" was the opening salvo, always met by a suspicious look, and a pause in chewing.

"What?"

"I'm sure you know someone was found dead in your camp this morning. Did you see or hear anything suspicious last night?"

The answers were always negative. The newbies appeared polite and not particularly interested. Neither of them probed any deeper after receiving a negative response. She hoped they didn't plan on becoming detectives. The answers from the residents were what she expected. If the woman in the nearest tent hadn't seen or heard anything, she was pretty sure no one else had, or if they had, would decline to share that information with the cops. She couldn't blame them. Cops were usually bad news if you were destitute and homeless.

She thanked McCall and Henderson, told them to show up at the team meeting in the morning, and headed for her car. She needed a glass of wine, a frozen pizza, and some mindless TV to take her mind off this case.

CHAPTER SIX

"DADDY, CAN WE ORDER PIZZA FOR DINNER?" ZOE looked up at him with her elfin features, her mouth set in a wide smile.

"I don't know, Princess. Let's ask your mother," Daniel said, as he hung his rain jacket on a hook near the door.

"I heard that," Hannah said, exiting the kitchen. "Not today. Emilia made chicken enchiladas and salad. I'm glad you're home early." She kissed his cheek.

"Brenda let me off the hook. She's doing today's paperwork."

Daniel entered the kitchen and sat down. Hannah brought the tray of enchiladas along with all the fixings to the table and everyone helped themselves.

"This is good, Mommy," Zoe said.

"Be sure to tell Emilia tomorrow," Hannah said. "It makes her happy when we appreciate her cooking." She shot Daniel a look, and tilted her head towards Zoe.

Daniel took a deep breath. There was a knot in the pit of his stomach.. He had to tell Zoe and he had no idea of how she might react. He couldn't put it off any longer.

"Zoe, I have a surprise for you. I didn't tell you sooner because I wasn't sure it would happen, but we're having a visitor next week."

Zoe looked up. "Grandma and Grandpa?"

Daniel shook his head. "It's a long story Princess. Many years ago, when I was in the army, and before I met your mother, I was friends with a nice lady who lived in Washington State. When your Mom and I went on our honeymoon, a few months ago, we met her again. It turned out that she owned the B&B where we stayed. She has a thirteen-year-old son, a boy named Josh, who is coming to spend the week with us. I never knew this until recently, because his mother and I lost touch, but Josh is my son too. So, you've got a big stepbrother."

Zoe's eyes were wide. "A brother? Will he want to play with me?"

"He can't wait to meet you."

Zoe looked thoughtful. "Will you still love me if you have Josh?"

Daniel glanced at Hannah. Zoe never hesitated to ask the hard questions. Sometimes he wished that Hannah would be as forthright with her fears and feelings.

He reached over and put an arm around Zoe. "You're my Princess, and I'll love you always. I hope that we'll all come to care about Josh, and that he'll feel the same about us, but no one will love you any less."

Zoe flashed him her smile. "We should all make him feel like part of our family," she announced. "I bet he's nervous about meeting us."

"I bet you're right," Daniel said.

"We'll be extra nice," Hannah added.

∼

After dinner, with Zoe working on her homework in the den, Hannah slid into Daniel's arms and hugged him. "You did that perfectly," she said.

"Thank goodness. After the day I've had, it's nice to get something right."

She looked up at him. "What happened today?"

"Brenda and I drove all over town, trying to ID a guy found murdered in a homeless encampment."

"Prints not in the system?"

"Don't have them yet. He was a trans man, so Brenda thought we should check out some of the transgender clinics that provide testosterone shots. She's really motivated to solve LGBT hate crimes. Unfortunately, none of the doctors recognized his photo."

Daniel walked over to the kitchen desk, where he'd dropped his file folder, and handed it to her.

Hannah took out the flyer and stared at it under the light, lips pursed and eyebrows drawn together. "Daniel, I know this man. He's my patient."

CHAPTER SEVEN

IT WAS FIVE MINUTES TO EIGHT WHEN HANNAH arrived at her office. As usual, it was empty and gloriously quiet. No conversation at the front desk or ringing phones, or noise from printers and the fax machine.

She walked past the exam areas and into her consultation room. This morning she had an extra item on her *To Do* list. She walked back to the storage area where they'd put the old paper charts. Each time a patient came in, their chart was scanned and transferred to the new computer system, and the paper chart was sent into long term storage. She worked her way through the C's and extracted the chart of Kevin Chase.

Returning to her desk, she opened it to the first page and texted his name, address and birth date to Daniel. Then she read slowly through her notes, mourning her patient.

Daniel was a few minutes late joining the team meeting, but he could tell that Brenda forgave him when he handed over a large box of doughnuts. Everyone helped themselves. She introduced Daniel to McCall and Henderson.

"They're new recruits to our station. They helped last night with the interviews at the homeless camp," she said.

"This is going to be a short meeting," she continued. "We're not much further along than we were yesterday. The homeless camp interviews were a bust. See no evil. Hear no evil. Speak no evil."

"Do you think they were telling the truth?" Daniel asked, "or did they just not want to get involved?"

"Both," Brenda said. "It's really noisy under the freeway and the rain didn't help. Unless someone was up and watching at four in the morning, I doubt anyone heard anything."

"Fingerprints?" Daniel asked.

"Bill sent them over this morning and said he'd have the autopsy results for us later today. We ran them through the system and got one hit: Kayla Chase, arrested for prostitution fifteen years ago in Hollywood. She was homeless at the time, so no address."

"I don't get it. I thought the vic was a guy," Henderson said.

"The victim was a transsexual," Brenda said.

Daniel glanced at the two men and saw poker faces.

"Never seen one of those before," McCall said. "So this arrest took place when he was a she?"

"Right,"

Daniel's phone pinged and he glanced at it. "Well, I have an update. The John Doe's name is Kevin Chase and I have his address and date of birth."

Brenda's jaw dropped. "You are kidding. How did you do that?"

"Hannah. She recognized his photo last night and said

he'd been her patient. My wife's a physician," Daniel explained to the rookies.

"Why didn't you call me?" Brenda asked. "It never fails to amaze me how many times Hannah has known, or taken care of, one of our murder victims."

"I tried calling but you didn't pick up."

"I was pretty wiped out last night. Why don't you and I go visit Kevin's place?" Brenda suggested. "You two officers can resume your regular patrol. We'll call you if we need extra help."

"Yeah, sure." The two rookies left the room.

"What's your impression of them?" Daniel asked.

Brenda shrugged. "Too early to tell. They follow orders and are careful not to voice their opinions in front of me. They weren't thrilled about being asked to stay past the end of their shifts, and I wasn't impressed by their interview technique. I'm withholding judgment until I get a better sense of whether they're going to work out. Where are we going?"

"Hollywood. The address is on Selma."

CHAPTER EIGHT

BRENDA DROVE THE BLACK AND WHITE THEY'D taken from the parking lot. Selma was a short street just south of Hollywood Blvd., running between Highland and Gower. Unlike bustling Hollywood, or Sunset to the south, it was populated by dingy apartment buildings, cracked sidewalks and an occasional motel. It was also within walking distance of the LGBT center. Brenda had patrolled it many times during her stint in the Hollywood station.

She pulled up in front of a shabby one-story building with a line of doors facing the street. It was a depressing place to live.

"Let's see if there's a manager on site," she said.

The door on the western edge of the building had a faded sign that said *Management.*

Brenda knocked.

"Yeah."

"Police. We need to ask a few questions." No point in scaring the guy.

The door opened, revealing a middle-aged, unshaven

man wearing baggy jeans and a dirty white T-shirt. A whiff of marijuana escaped the apartment.

Brenda showed her badge. "You have a tenant named Kevin Chase?"

"Two doors down. He in trouble?"

"Unfortunately, he was found dead on Monday morning. We need to search his apartment and talk to everyone in the building." Brenda said.

"Who would want to kill Kevin? He never bothered no one."

"Tell me about him. How long has he been living here?" Brenda took out a small notebook and pen from her pocket.

"I been here five years and he was living here then. Most of the tenants come and go, but Kevin stayed. He was nice, polite, and gave me no trouble. Always paid his rent on time."

"Was he friendly with any of the other tenants?" Daniel asked.

The manager shrugged. "It's not a friendly building. Most people keep to themselves. I never saw Kevin talking to anybody."

"Did you ever see him having visitors?"

"I think he had a girlfriend. I saw the same woman go into his place a couple a times. He went out a lot at night. Don't know where. None of my business where the tenants go."

"Can you describe his girlfriend?" Brenda asked.

"She was black, sexy, tall. Didn't really see her face but she wore short, tight dresses and had a nice ass. All I can tell you."

"She drive a car?" Daniel asked.

"Didn't see one. He didn't have one neither."

"Thanks," Brenda said. "I need the names of your other tenants and a key to Kevin's apartment."

The apartment was a studio, the size of a college dorm room. It made Brenda sad to look at it. The bed was a single, sloppily made. The closet was a cubbyhole covered with a curtain. It contained several pairs of worn jeans, a denim jacket, a worn terrycloth robe and an assortment of shirts. There were several pairs of sneakers and a scuffed pair of black loafers. Brenda checked the pockets. Empty. The dresser contained underwear, socks and a few sweaters.

The kitchen nook had a mini-refrigerator, a sink and a microwave. The freezer held two frozen dinners. The refrigerator contained milk, a few beers, half a loaf of packaged bread, and some chunky peanut butter. The one kitchen cabinet had a few plastic plates and bowls, and boxes of cereal and crackers.

Daniel checked under the mattress and opened the drawer of the bedside table.

"Anything?" Brenda asked.

"Bills, paid and pending." He held up a package of envelopes held together with a rubber band. "And..." Daniel smiled. "A cell phone."

Brenda gave him a thumbs up and went into the tiny bathroom. The shower was the size of a phone booth and the towels were threadbare. The medicine cabinet, however, yielded a box of 4-milligram testosterone patches. The prescribing physician was Robert Ryan MD, the doctor in charge of the LGBT Center transgender clinic.

"I think we're finished here. Let's split up and knock on the doors of the remaining tenants, and see if we can learn anything useful. Then we can go back to the LGBT Center and talk to Doctor Ryan," Brenda said.

"Or, when we're done here, we can drop off the phone at the station, ask Izzy to hack the passcode, and see if we can get a few names of people who knew him. We could phone Ryan from the station. Kill two birds with one stone?" Daniel suggested.

Brenda nodded. "How about we get lunch first? My treat."

A detour to Canter's and a hot pastrami sandwich improved Brenda's mood considerably, as did the autopsy report which arrived, as promised, by the Coroner.

She removed it from the printer, and studied it. "Cause of death was a subdural hematoma, secondary to a skull fracture. The fracture pattern suggests the weapon was a pipe. Before he died, he was beaten. There are a considerable number of pre-mortem injuries all over his body, as well as bleeding from the kidneys and spleen. The lividity pattern suggests he died where we found him," she said.

"Hard to believe anyone would miss a beating of that magnitude in the camp," Daniel said. "My guess is he was beaten elsewhere, and dumped there to die."

"I agree," Brenda said. "He doesn't seem to have had any of the transgender surgeries. Still had breasts and female genitals, but he had a hysterectomy and ovaries removed."

"Interesting. I wonder if Hannah did the hysterectomy and why."

"I'm going to give her a call and see if we can talk later today. I want to see what she knows about him."

"I think you should do that interview without me,"

Daniel said. "I don't want some defense attorney trying to exclude her evidence because she's married to me."

"You're right," Brenda said. "Why don't you drop off the phone with Izzy, and once he cracks the passcode see what you can find out about people in his address book. Following up on that can be our project for tomorrow."

CHAPTER NINE

H ANNAH SUGGESTED THAT BRENDA COME TO HER office at four o'clock, when she was finished with her patients.

Brenda had never been there before. She paused in the waiting room. The scent of roses permeated the air. Comfortable chairs, upholstered in pale turquoise were centered by a glass coffee table with a driftwood base. The room exuded tranquility.

Hannah greeted her with a smile and escorted her into the consultation room. Hannah's private space faced north with a view of the hills.

"Your office is gorgeous," Brenda commented as she sat down.

"Glad you like it. I wish you were here for a happier purpose."

"Me too," Brenda said. "Daniel told me Kevin Chase was your patient, and the autopsy showed he'd had a hysterectomy. Were you the doctor who did it?"

Hannah nodded. "About ten years ago."

"I know you aren't supposed to reveal medical information, and I'm not asking for it. What I really want to know is anything you can tell me about the kind of person he was, and any details you might know about his life that could help us find out who did this. How did he happen to come to you as a patient?"

Hannah leaned back in her chair and fiddled with her pen, avoiding Brenda's gaze. "Daniel told me you were committed to solving this case, and I understand why. An LGBT hate crime must feel like an assault on your community. I'd feel the same if it was an anti-Semitic murder. I'll share the story, but I have to confess that I'm embarrassed at how I reacted when I first met Kevin. I'd never encountered a trans male before and didn't know what to make of him."

"That's not surprising," Brenda said. "Trans people, especially trans men, have been virtually invisible. No one talked about them back then, and there were hardly any trans characters in the media."

Hannah finally put down the pen and made eye contact. "I came back from lunch one day, and there was a black man, with a beard, sitting in my waiting room. I assumed he was someone's husband or boyfriend. Then my receptionist came into my office and said that the man claimed to have been referred by the emergency room, and had an appointment with me under the name Kayla Chase. She was worried he might be mentally ill or dangerous."

"Were you worried too?" Brenda asked.

"I confess, I was. I told her to bring him into my consult room, but to leave the door open, and to ask building security to come upstairs and wait, just in case I needed them."

"What happened next?" Brenda asked.

"Once I started talking to him, and he gave me his referral papers from the emergency room, everything made sense. It would have been nice if the ER had given me the heads up, so I wouldn't have felt like a fool."

"Cut yourself some slack, Hannah. Gynecologists aren't used to seeing guys in their waiting rooms. Why did he want to see you?" Brenda asked.

"He told me that he was a female-to-male transsexual with anemia and heavy bleeding. The ER docs had diagnosed a large fibroid uterus. Most of the time, testosterone therapy stops a woman's periods, but not when there are big fibroids. So, I operated on him."

"He wasn't coming to you for hormone therapy?"

Hannah shook her head. "He was getting that elsewhere. I wouldn't have had any idea of the proper dose for him."

"What kind of a person was he? Did you like him?"

"I did. He told me he went by the name Kevin, and he seemed very kind and gentle. He tried to make me comfortable, when I should have been the one making him feel accepted and welcome."

Hannah was such a warm person, she probably had been her usual smiling self, once she understood the situation.

"I'm sure you did. That's who you are," Brenda said.

"Being nice isn't enough. I made a stupid mistake when I admitted him to the hospital. If I'd been thinking clearly, I'd have gotten him a bed on the general surgery floor, where there are patients of all genders. Instead, I just automatically admitted him to gynecology for his post-operative care."

"Did someone make him feel like a misfit?" Brenda asked. She could visualize some transphobic behavior on the part of staff.

"I don't think so, but he was afraid the nurses would freak out, seeing a man, so he shaved his beard and put on a pink nightgown for the occasion. At the time, I just thought he was being considerate. I didn't realize until much later, when transgender care began to enter the medical mainstream, that I was the one who had screwed up. He should never have had to do that. I still feel guilty about it."

"Has it entered the medical mainstream?"

"Our hospital hired a full-time surgeon who does gender-affirming surgery, and care for trans men and women has become part of the residency curriculum, so I'd say yes, but ten years ago, doctors were oblivious."

That was reassuring. Transgender awareness certainly hadn't yet penetrated the LAPD.

"Did you see him after the surgery?"

"He was my patient for ten years. I just saw him two months ago."

"You must have done something right then, Hannah. I doubt he'd have kept coming back if he didn't like you. Did he ever tell you anything personal?"

"Sometimes. He'd had a difficult and marginalized life. He told me he lived in an SRO hotel in Hollywood, and was on disability. He'd come in occasionally because he'd had sexual encounters that hadn't ended well, and he'd been beaten, or needed STD testing. Recently, though, he did mention having a girlfriend. I don't know her name."

"I don't suppose you have any idea of who might have wanted to kill him?" Brenda asked.

Hannah shook her head. "Not really, unless he picked a dangerous sexual partner, or was targeted by some right-wing transphobe. He was a good person, which is why I feel so awful about what happened."

"You wouldn't have an emergency notification listed for him?" Brenda asked. "Any family?"

Hannah opened a chart and looked. "I'm sorry. No one is listed. Trans people are often disowned by their families. He never mentioned any family ties, but you could check a birth certificate and see what you can find."

"I will. Thanks, Hannah. I hear you and Daniel are taking some vacation time next week. Enjoy it."

"Thanks. I'm really glad that you're in charge of this investigation. I know you'll try your hardest."

Brenda was planning on it. She was also hoping that Kevin's phone would give her some new avenues to investigate.

CHAPTER TEN

THE NEXT MORNING, DANIEL SAT AT HIS DESK WITH a printout of Kevin Chase's contacts. They painted a picture of a very constrained life, a Redwood tree planted in a bonsai container. There were addresses and phone numbers of clinics, doctors (including Hannah), pharmacies, supermarkets, bars and the occasional service person (plumber and electrician). Personal names and numbers were few and far between. Prominently missing were any contacts with the last name Chase. He seemed to have been someone always eating alone in a restaurant, or observing a crowded room through a window.

Daniel found a birth certificate under the name Kayla Chase and the names of his parents, Shavon and Tenisha Chase. Kevin had been born in 1974 in Inglewood. Checking a few databases, he determined that both parents were still alive and at the same address. Google street view showed a well-kept, one-story home.

Glancing up, he saw that Brenda had arrived. She was dressed in one of her interview outfits, black slacks and a matching blazer with a white shirt. Waving at him, she walked over to their adjacent desks.

"I've found Kevin's parents," Daniel said. "Notifying them is probably the first thing we should do this morning. Hopefully, they'll claim his body."

"Don't get your hopes up," Brenda said. "Were his parents listed in his phone contacts?"

"No, nothing under the name Chase. I did track down two women and a man, listed on his phone, who seemed to be personal contacts. He also had a few trans bars listed. We can start checking those out after we go to Inglewood. I've never seen a phone with so few names."

"Hannah really liked him," Brenda said. "She was very upset about his murder."

"I know. Was she able to give you any useful information?"

"Only that he seems to have had some risky sexual encounters. Given the fact that he was arrested for prostitution, apparently before he transitioned, he may have continued with dangerous hook-ups as a man. She did mention he'd told her he had a girlfriend. I wonder if that was the woman the apartment manager mentioned."

Daniel shrugged. "Possible. We'll find out eventually. I'm hoping we make some significant progress before I take time off this coming week."

"I'm sure I can handle it."

"I know you can. You're an outstanding detective."

Her face lit up.

"I guess we should get going," Brenda retrieved two doughnuts from the adjacent conference room, and handed one to him. "Your turn to drive."

~

The Chase home was painted a sky blue with white trim, and had large pots of geraniums on the front steps. The neighborhood seemed solidly middle class: mowed lawns, fresh paint, occasional swing sets and basketball hoops. As Daniel parked the police car, Brenda replaced her phone in her purse and mentally rehearsed what she would say.

"I hate this, more than any other part of police work, telling the family that someone has died."

"I've seen you do it many times," Daniel said. "You're always empathic and tactful."

"The problem is that I have no idea how these parents will react. It's complicated when your child is transgender."

"Just be your kind self. It'll be okay."

The two of them rang the bell, and the door was opened a sliver, with the chain attached, by a gray-haired woman with multiple long braids, in a bright, cotton print dress.

"Mrs. Tenisha Chase?" Brenda asked.

"Yes."

"I'm Detective Jordan and this is Detective Ross." Brenda showed her badge. "May we come in for a moment? We have some news about your son, Kevin."

"I don't have no son," she said, beginning to close the door.

Brenda pushed back on it with her hand. "Kayla."

The woman's mouth tightened. "One minute." She closed the door, removed the chain lock and reopened it. "Come in."

They were escorted into a neat living room and told to sit on the sofa. A dark-skinned, burly, white-haired man in his sixties was seated in a recliner. He looked up through a pair of glasses as they entered.

"This is my husband, Shavon. These are the cops. They have something to tell us about Kayla." She seated herself on the remaining chair with her arms crossed over her chest.

"If she's in trouble, don't come to us. She left this family fifteen years ago when she decided she'd rather be a man. It's against God's law, and we are God-fearing people." Shavon glared at Brenda.

"I'm sorry to bring you bad news, but Kayla was found dead Monday morning in West Los Angeles. We are treating the death as a homicide," Brenda said.

Tenisha winced, and a tear rolled down her cheek. Her husband maintained a poker face.

"I warned her that she'd come to no good, going to Hollywood, being with queers and degenerates. What kind of a life is that for a nice girl from a church-going family? Her mother and I worked hard to give her a happy life. We wanted her to have a husband and children and an education."

The pitch of his voice rose. It cracked as he broke down. Brenda didn't know what to say. She glanced around the room, looking for family photos. There were none. There was an elaborate cross hung over the fireplace, several framed needlepoint pictures with Bible verses, and a color-ful, handmade quilt on the wall over the sofa.

"The coroner has finished the autopsy," Daniel said. "You can claim the body whenever you wish."

Shavon spoke up. "We don't wish. She's no part of our family."

Tenisha asked. "What happens to her if we don't claim the body?"

"The county cremates unclaimed bodies," Brenda explained, "and once a year they have a ceremony and bury the ashes on county property."

Tenisha turned to her husband. "We should talk in private. We'll let you know?"

Daniel nodded. "Take your time." He handed her a card with the Coroner's information. "Please call this number when you've made a decision. Is there any other family who might want to claim the body? Siblings perhaps?"

"Kayla was our only child." More tears were rolling down Tenisha's face.

Brenda and Daniel stood up. Brenda could tell that Kevin's parents were about to have an argument. She hoped that Tenisha would win, and give Kevin the respect of a decent burial.

"We'll leave you now," Brenda said. "We're sorry to be the bearers of such bad news."

CHAPTER ELEVEN

"THAT DIDN'T GO VERY WELL," BRENDA SAID AS THEY walked toward the car.

"I think you were as kind and tactful as you could have been. It's not our job to fix family estrangement." Daniel used the remote to unlock the doors, and Brenda slid into the passenger seat. She was enveloped in a black, smoky cloud of depression.

Daniel started the engine but didn't put the car in gear. "You look glum. What are you thinking?"

Brenda exhaled and said nothing.

Daniel waited.

"I was just wondering, if I was killed in the line of duty, whether my parents would refuse to claim the body of their degenerate lesbian daughter."

"Have you come out to them?"

"No. I keep thinking it's time, and I keep procrastinating. When I do, there won't be a happy ending."

"I promise, if you get killed in the line of duty, the LAPD will give you a hero's funeral, and I'll be in the adjacent coffin because we're a team"

Brenda laughed. Daniel always managed to cheer her up. She couldn't have been paired with a nicer partner.

"Seriously, Daniel, if I died, Marcy couldn't claim my body. We're just roommates."

"Do you want to do something about that?"

"Like get married?"

"You've been living together for awhile. Is Marcy the one? Gay marriage is legal now in California."

The thought of Marcy brought an instant feeling of warmth, like being wrapped in a down comforter; her smile, her kindness, her sense of humor, the fact that she did something for a living that had nothing to do with danger and dead bodies. When Brenda came home to Marcy, no matter how stressful her day had been, her blood pressure dropped twenty points. Marcy had made their apartment a true home. The thought of marriage had crossed her mind, but it would mean coming out to her parents and at work. She hadn't quite gotten up her courage yet.

"She is for me. I hope the feeling is mutual. It still bothers me that we could marry in California, and our marriage would be invalid as soon as we crossed the state line."

"I don't blame you, but being married in California is better than not being married at all."

Daniel finally pulled out of their parking space.

"Has it made a difference to you and Hannah? You lived together as long as we have."

"The sense of commitment is more complete. You know that whatever the problem is, you have to work hard to solve it together. Breaking up is the last resort. For me, I also finally feel like Zoe's dad, and that makes me happy."

"I've always thought the two of you were a great fit," Brenda said. "By the way, where are we going?"

"West Hollywood. There's a woman we need to interview about Kevin."

"The one in his contacts?"

"Right. Her name is Dolly Divine."

"Seriously? That sounds like a stage name."

"I thought so too," Daniel said, "but it isn't. She's trans, and she changed her name legally. I looked it up. Dolly works as a singer and part-time bartender at a trans bar in Hollywood, not far from where Kevin was living."

"Makes sense," Brenda said. "Changing your name is part of the process of claiming your true gender."

"You seem well versed in the trans culture," Daniel said.

"I was a rookie at Hollywood station, and met a number of trans women while doing my job. I rescued one from an assault, and word went out that I was a cop who could be trusted. Then I met more of them. I didn't know many trans men. They blend in better and are somewhat less likely to be victims. I wonder if Dolly is the woman the apartment manager mentioned."

Daniel shrugged. "Could be. We'll find out when we talk to her."

Brenda glanced at her watch. "If she works at a bar, she may still be asleep at this hour. How about we stop somewhere for lunch before we wake her up?" Brenda was feeling better. Hunger was a good sign.

After a plate of shwarma, hummus and pita at a Lebanese restaurant, Brenda and Daniel pulled up in front of a midcentury apartment building in West Hollywood. A gate led into a courtyard, planted with olive trees and beds of drought-resistant plants. There were a few outdoor tables and chairs, unoccupied at this early afternoon hour. The building was two stories and the doors to the units surrounded the courtyard. There was a directory just inside the gate.

"Not much security," Daniel said. "The gate wasn't even locked."

Brenda scanned the directory. D. Divine was in apartment 201. It was a corner unit.

The two of them climbed the stairs, and Brenda rang the bell. It was a Ring doorbell with video and motion detector.

"Who is it?"

Brenda held her badge in front of the camera. "I'm Detective Jordan of the LAPD. This is Detective Ross. We wanted to ask you a few questions about Kevin Chase."

"Oh my God. Is Kevin in trouble?"

Not a question Brenda wanted to answer through a closed door.

"Could we please talk inside?"

There was a sound of locks being undone and the door opened.

"Come in."

Dolly Divine was gorgeous. She stood almost six feet tall, wearing a red silk wrap-around robe which displayed a curvaceous body. Her features suggested North African ancestry, perhaps Ethiopian or Somalian, and she wore her hair in a long afro. Her eyes were open wide with fear. The scent of coffee wafted through the door.

The apartment was sparsely furnished but colorful and unique with pillows and fabrics in African patterns, and a display of primitive art, masks and sculpture.

Dolly had been in the midst of breakfast when they arrived, and she asked them to sit at her kitchen table.

"What happened to Kevin?" She put down her mug,

clasping her hands tightly together, bracing herself for bad news.

"Are you a good friend?"

"I'm his girlfriend."

"I'm so sorry. Kevin was found dead Monday morning in a homeless encampment in West LA. We're investigating his death as a homicide."

Dolly's hands covered her face and her body began to shake. There was no sound, as if she was holding back her cries, not wanting to lose it in front of cops. Brenda and Daniel waited quietly for her to regain control. When she finally looked up, her cheeks were wet.

"Can you think of anyone who would have a reason to kill Kevin?" Daniel asked.

"Sure. He was trans. Our existence is a reason to kill us. Do you have any idea of how many trans people are murdered every year?"

"I do," Brenda said, "and I know how few of these hate crimes are solved."

She leaned forward and made eye contact with Dolly. "I'm in charge of this investigation and I promise you, I will do everything possible to find Kevin's killer. Will you help me?"

"How?"

"First of all, tell me, when was the last time you saw him?"

"Sunday night. He came into the bar to hear me sing. I perform around 11 PM and work behind the bar until it closes at 2 a.m. Kevin is something of a morning person, so we don't usually spend the night together when I'm on the late shift. He left around midnight, and we made plans to see one another the next day. I'm off Mondays and Tuesdays."

"Were you worried when he didn't show up on Monday?" Daniel asked.

"At first I was pissed off. When he was an hour late, which is totally not like him, I tried calling, but my calls went to voicemail. I finally went over to his apartment, but he wasn't there either."

"Did you go in?"

"Yeah, I have his keys. No sign that he'd slept there or had breakfast. Then I started to worry."

"Did you consider reporting him missing?" Brenda asked.

"No offense, but the trans community doesn't have much faith or trust in the cops. I checked everywhere I could think of to see if anyone had seen him: the LGBT Center where he gets his hormones and attends a trans group, his supermarket, the restaurants I know he likes. No one had seen him that day. I decided that if I didn't hear from him by today, I would consider the cops, and then you guys showed up."

"Miss Divine, does your bar have security cameras inside and out?" Daniel asked.

"Yeah. We're on Highland Avenue. Most of the businesses have cameras. There's a high crime rate."

"We need the name of the manager," Brenda said. "We have to see those tapes. Maybe we can trace Kevin's movements."

"The bar isn't open now, but I can call the manager for you and have him meet you there."

"That would be very helpful. Does Kevin have any friends we could talk to?"

Dolly smiled. "Not many. Kevin was so shy. I remember when he first came to the bar. He was so good looking, but he just sat on a barstool, drank Pepsi, and listened to me sing. He never talked to anyone. I finally broke the silence and came on to him, but I had to make all the first moves. He does have a few friends he's made in the trans group. I can give you their names and numbers."

She got up from the table, found her phone and wrote two names and phone numbers on a scrap of paper. "The first one is his therapist. You might want to talk to her first."

Daniel stood up. "You've been very helpful. If you could make that call now, we'll head over to your bar. We might want to talk to you again, depending on what we learn."

"Is there anyone you'd like me to call for you, a friend or family member? It helps not to be alone after getting such bad news," Brenda asked.

Dolly shook her head. "I have friends I can call to come over." She leaned toward Brenda. "Are you really gonna work this case?"

"You have my word," Brenda handed Dolly her card. Please call me, any time, if you think of anything else that could be important."

CHAPTER TWELVE

T HE BAR WAS CALLED TRANSFORMATION, AND IT WAS wedged between a dry cleaners and a Juice bar. A sign on the bar entrance said: *Closed. Open 7 p.m. to 2 a.m.* But when Daniel knocked, the door was opened by a short, stocky, very muscular guy wearing a wifebeater shirt and sleeve tattoos. He had a shaved head and a round face with a sparse beard.

"You the cops?"

Daniel held out his badge.

"I'm Stan, the manager. Come on in." He held open the door and locked it after they entered.

The bar was small and dim. At the far end was a round stage with dingy red velvet curtains. The floor was covered in octagonal black and white tile, dating from the thirties. A dark wood counter with bar stools, and a bunch of small tables, constituted the seating. There was a large mirror behind the bar, creating an illusion of space. Bottles of whiskey were arranged on two sets of shelves on either side. An unlit disco ball hung from the ceiling.

Stan pulled up a chair and motioned to them. Daniel and Brenda sat down.

"Dolly said her boy Kevin was killed Sunday night. How can I help?"

"Did you know him?" Brenda asked.

"I knew who he was. Dolly took a liking to him. He wasn't the social type. Just sat there, nursed his drink and watched her sing."

"Did you notice him leaving Sunday night?"

"Not really. I don't keep track of who comes and goes."

"Dolly said you have security cameras," Daniel said.

"That we do." Stan pointed out two cameras, one near the door, the other focused on the hall to the bathrooms. "We also got one outside."

"I'll need the recordings from all three of them Sunday night and Monday morning, till one p.m.," Brenda said.

"They're on my computer, in the back. You got a flash drive? I'll copy them for you."

Daniel glanced at Brenda. It hadn't occurred to him that he might need a flash drive.

She reached into her pants pocket, raised her eyebrows, and handed one to Stan. He took it and headed toward his computer. Brenda followed.

"How come you had a USB stick with you?" Daniel asked, as they left the bar.

"Welcome to the 21st century. I would no more forget to take one of these than I would forget to put on my gun. You should make a point of carrying one with you. I won't always be there to save the day." She grinned at him.

Daniel knew his way around a computer, but compared

to Brenda and some of the younger detectives, he was a Luddite.

"I called our rookies, McCall and Henderson, and told them to drive over here and meet us. I'm going to have them canvass all the businesses on the block and collect the outside camera footage."

The block held several clothing stores including one specializing in kinky lingerie, a jeans store, and a thrift shop. There were also the usual fast food suspects, Starbucks, fried chicken and tacos. A fifties diner anchored the corner.

"Most of the stores close well before midnight so I doubt anyone saw or heard anything, but maybe we can trace Kevin's movements," Brenda said.

"Good thinking. After they get here, how about we head back to the station and go home. We're both tired and we need to be able to concentrate to review all those videos."

"I could use an early night," Brenda agreed.

As she opened the door of their apartment, Brenda could smell the enticing scent of roast chicken. Marcy was whipping up some mashed potatoes to go with it. Her dark pixie cut framed her face. Brenda envied her tall stature and seemingly effortless slim figure.

"You must have read my mind," Brenda said. "I'm starving."

"Did your mind want a cocktail before dinner? I could make us some Aperol spritzers." She put down the bowl of mashed potatoes and leaned over to give Brenda a thoroughly satisfying kiss.

Brenda relaxed against her soft body. "Just what I needed."

"Go sit on the couch with your feet up and I'll be in with our drinks."

Marcy headed to the refrigerator. At that moment, Brenda's phone rang.

"Damn, it's my mother." Brenda took the phone into the living room.

Marcy followed five minutes later, with two ice cold cocktails. Brenda was stretched out on the sofa. Marcy handed her a glass and she took a large swallow.

"Something wrong, babe?"

"Not really. My parents are coming in tomorrow for their annual physicals, and want to take me to dinner. I'm not up for it. This case is exhausting and stressful, and all I want to do after work is have a drink and dinner with you in front of the TV. Anyway, I have to meet them in Beverly Hills at the Cheesecake Factory."

"Want me to come with you? Your parents seem to like me, and my being there might help deflect any questions you don't want to answer."

"You're really willing to go to dinner with my parents? They do like you but they think you're my roommate."

"I'm here to support you. Besides, you know how much I love cheesecake."

Brenda considered. They'd been together for almost two years and she still couldn't get up the nerve to tell her parents that her charming, smart, successful roommate was her partner. When they'd visited her new apartment, she'd closed the door to the bedrooms so they wouldn't question the queen-sized bed, or see that the second bedroom was used as Marcy's design studio.

"Marcy, I know it's time for me to come out to them. I just keep hoping that they won't freak because they see how wonderful you are."

"I want you to live honestly, but you'll tell them when you're ready."

Brenda got up from the sofa and gave Marcy a prolonged hug. "Thanks for being so understanding. You are the best, and I love you."

CHAPTER THIRTEEN

WELL FED AND RESTED, BRENDA ARRIVED AT THE station and plugged the flash drive into her computer. She fast forwarded until she saw Kevin arrive at 10:37 p.m. on the outside camera. A wave of sadness crashed over her. Kevin looked so vibrant, attractive and alive. He was smiling and relaxed as he entered the bar, wearing the same jeans and leather jacket that clothed his dead body.

Brenda switched to the inside camera and watched as Kevin took a seat at the bar, accepted a drink and a kiss on the cheek from Dolly, and watched as Dolly performed for half an hour at 11:00 p.m. As she watched Dolly's body language, Brenda regretted that the security cameras had no audio. She would have liked to hear Dolly sing.

The bar was only half full on that Sunday night, and after Dolly's performance people drifted out. Kevin didn't interact with anyone but Dolly, and no one seemed to pay any attention to him. At five minutes before midnight, he walked back to the men's room, and then blew a kiss at Dolly and left.

"Detective Jordan."

Brenda turned to see Henderson. He handed her two flash drives. "This one's for the east side of Highland. The other one has the stores to the west. Some of them had exterior cameras so we've got footage of most of the block, from 10 p.m. to 2 a.m., as you asked. You want us to help you review them?"

"Good job," Brenda said, accepting the sticks. "Detective Ross should be in any minute, so the two of us will slog through these. Thanks for the offer. We'll probably need your help again once we figure out our next moves."

"You seem to be spending a lot of time on this tranny," Henderson said.

"I'm doing my job the best way I know how," Brenda said. A flash of anger made her face feel hot. This was the kind of guy who would refer to her as a dyke if she came out at work, no doubt behind her back since she outranked him. The LAPD needed to do a better job screening out candidates who were racist or homophobic. No one should have to put up with that crap.

"Good morning." Daniel arrived, carrying a bag and smiling. "I figured if we were going to be welded to our desks this morning, we needed bagels and cream cheese."

"My hero."

Daniel set out the bagels on his desk. Henderson immediately grabbed one and left the room.

"What have you got so far?"

"Not much. I reviewed the interior cameras. Kevin's only interaction was with Dolly. No one seemed to pay any attention to him. I was just about to switch to the outside camera. Henderson gave me video from all the stores on the block. This is the east side of the street. Kevin left the bar at eleven fifty-five. Let's see if we can follow him."

Daniel saw Kevin leave and walk south on Highland. He paused the video, and checked a map on Google.

"Brenda, Kevin isn't heading home. Selma is to the north and he's walking in the opposite direction. I wonder where he's headed."

Brenda got up and looked over Daniel's shoulder. He replayed Kevin's movements and let the video continue. They lost him after he crossed Lexington.

"Santa Monica and Highland is the center of male prostitution in this area. I wonder if he's buying or selling?" Brenda said.

"Should we go check it out?"

"No one will be there at this hour, but yes. We definitely will need to speak to the hookers."

"There's something that doesn't make sense to me," Daniel said. "Assuming that Kevin was killed in Hollywood, why move him and take him all the way to the Westside? Why not just leave him in an alley somewhere? It would probably be hours before the body was discovered. Why take the trouble and risk being seen dumping him under the freeway?"

"That's a really good point. Maybe figuring it out will lead us to the killers. We should finish going through the rest of these videos. I need to be home no later than six."

"Hot date?" Daniel asked.

"Dinner with my parents. Command performance," Brenda said. "And I'm bringing Marcy."

CHAPTER FOURTEEN

T HE CHEESECAKE FACTORY, AS USUAL, WAS NOISY and crowded, but her mother had made a reservation, so the four of them had a booth toward the back of the restaurant. Marcy looked great in a royal blue leather jacket, slim black pants and knee-high, soft leather boots. She'd even put on makeup for the occasion.

Brenda had inherited her looks from her mother, Faith, who was short and curvy with blonde hair, blue eyes, and a pert nose. After three kids, her hair had turned gray, and she'd put on a good deal of weight, but she still had the same warm smile. Brenda's father, James, looked like the police chief he was: serious, dignified and reserved. Her two older brothers were in law enforcement, but Brenda still wasn't sure if her father was proud to have a daughter in the LAPD, or agreed with her mother that she should marry, settle down and have a brood of kids.

"You remember my roommate, Marcy Adams," Brenda said.

"Of course I do. I love your outfit. I wish Brenda had your flair for fashion," Faith said.

"Thanks so much for including me," Marcy said, as she ducked the motherly comment. "I rarely get to indulge my passion for cheesecake. My parents live in Phoenix, so I'm not lucky enough to have frequent dinners with them the way Brenda can."

Brenda could tell by the expression on her mother's face that Marcy had made a hit.

"How is your work, Marcy? As I recall, you're an interior designer. That's a nice, civilized job for a young lady," Faith said. "No dead bodies." She turned toward her daughter. "You look tired, dear."

"I am," Brenda said. "I've got a particularly difficult case right now."

She'd caught her father's attention. His eyebrows rose. "Tell me about it."

"It's a hate crime. A trans man was found dead in a homeless camp. He'd been left there after a beating to bleed to death from a brain hemorrhage. These cases are particularly difficult because the killer rarely knows the victim and the motive isn't personal. Unless you luck out with the trace evidence, it can be impossible to solve."

Faith wrinkled her nose. "What's a trans man?" she asked.

"Did you ever see the movie 'Boys Don't Cry?' trans men are people who are born with a woman's body, but who know, in their minds, that they are supposed to have been male, and who transition with hormones and sometimes surgery."

"That's disgusting," Faith said.

"The hate crime?" Brenda asked, already knowing the answer.

"No, destroying your God-given woman's body and pretending to be a man."

"Fortunately," her father added, "we don't have that kind of murder in West Covina. It's not Hollywood. Why waste your time trying to find out who murdered some deviant?"

Brenda's rage was building. Under the table she dug her fingers into Marcy's thigh. "Because it's my job, and because every victim deserves the dignity of a full investigation."

Her father shrugged. "I think your time in Hollywood exposed you to too many pansies and dykes. Myself, I prefer to focus on protecting our fine, church-going, Christian citizens, people with values."

Marcy squeezed Brenda's hand and smiled at her parents. "We have a rule at our apartment. No police talk over dinner. Why don't we order? I'm starved."

By the time the meal was over, with Marcy masterfully steering the conversation to amusing shows on Netflix, Brenda's anger had subsided. It had been replaced with sadness.

Marcy drove home. "I understand why you haven't been anxious for me to spend time with your parents," Marcy said.

"This was a revelation," Brenda said. "I'd always assumed they believed that homosexuality was a sin, because it said so in the Bible. We never discussed it and I'd never heard them express such bigotry. I've been avoiding telling them I was a lesbian in the hope that cultural change would make them more open-minded and make coming out easier for me. I didn't want to lose their love."

Marcy reached over and caressed Brenda's cheek. "I know, babe."

"I've finally realized that their minds won't ever change.

When I come out, they'll probably disown me, and I don't care." Tears were spilling from her eyes, and her voice cracked.

"Obviously there's a part of you that does care. Otherwise you'd have told them a long time ago. Believe me, I know exactly how you feel. I've been there."

"I can't do this anymore. I have to be myself. I can't change who they are and what they believe, but I've let those beliefs rule me. No more"

Marcy stopped at a red light, leaned over and kissed her. "It's about time."

"And I'm going to solve that murder, whatever it takes."

CHAPTER FIFTEEN

H ANNAH WAS PULLING TOGETHER A QUICK breakfast on Friday morning.

"Any progress on Kevin's murder?" Hannah poured two mugs of coffee, and took out some jam and butter from the refrigerator.

"Yes and no."

"What can you share?" She knew Daniel wasn't supposed to talk about cases in progress, but he'd made exceptions before when she knew the victim.

Daniel sat down at the breakfast table and cut a slice of challah. "We've interviewed his girlfriend, and gotten surveillance videos from every store on Highland Avenue, where he was last seen."

"Learn anything?"

"He was walking south, around midnight, toward Santa Monica Boulevard. It's an area where male prostitutes hang out. We're wondering if he was trying to get picked up. He was arrested for prostitution fifteen years ago, before he transitioned, but there's no record of anything since."

"Prostitution might explain the frequent STDs I've treated him for, and the bruising I've noticed. Prostitutes of all genders are at risk for violence. Maybe he went somewhere with a man who didn't know he was trans, and was furious when he found out."

Daniel took a bite of his bread, now liberally spread with butter and blueberry jam, and chewed. Hannah waited.

"There are several peculiar things about this case. We're puzzled about why the killers moved him to a homeless camp under the 405. Why not just let the body stay in Hollywood?"

"Maybe they thought the West LA police would call it an accident and not bother trying to solve it. Without an ID, finding the site of the killing would have been impossible. The police at the Hollywood station would have more experience with trans hate crimes and might work harder to find the killer."

"That's a good thought. Clearly they didn't reckon with Brenda. No one could have worked harder on this case."

"Are you still okay with taking next week off?"

He'd better be. Hannah wasn't going to be left by herself with a thirteen-year-old boy she barely knew.

"Of course. It's her case, and she can always call me if she needs to pick my brain."

"So, when is Josh scheduled to land?" Hannah asked.

"Can I come with you to pick him up?" Zoe, dressed for school and carrying her backpack, entered the kitchen.

Hannah gave her a hug and poured milk into Zoe's bowl of granola.

"I don't see why not," Daniel said. "His plane lands at two in the afternoon, tomorrow."

"He and I can plan fun things to do this week," Zoe said. "Do you think he'll like me?"

Daniel stood up, ready to head for work, and planted a kiss on her forehead. "How could anyone not like you?"

CHAPTER SIXTEEN

B RENDA WAS ALREADY AT HER DESK WHEN DANIEL walked into the station. He was hoping they'd learn something useful today. He was feeling guilty about taking next week off, but Josh had to be his priority.

"What's the plan for today? I don't suppose we've got any forensics back?"

Brenda rolled her eyes. "Of course not. Maybe we'll have something by Monday. I'm not hopeful. I doubt the killer left us fingerprints. This morning, you and I are going back to the LGBT center. I've arranged for us to interview Dr. Ryan and Esther Avila, the group leader for Kevin's trans group. Ryan called me a few days ago to identify Kevin, but Hannah beat him to it."

"Esther Avila is the name of the other woman in Kevin's phone," Daniel said.

Brenda nodded. "I hope she can help, and won't cite professional confidentiality."

"If she's a licensed therapist, confidentiality continues after death."

"I know," Brenda sighed. "All we can do is try."

~

When they arrived at the Center, Brenda suggested they split up and Daniel interview Dr. Joseph Ryan.

"HIPPA regulations will prohibit him from telling you anything medical, but maybe he knows a few things about Kevin's personal life," she suggested. "I'll talk to Esther."

Esther Avila was a plump, middle-aged Latina with a warm smile and long dark hair. Brenda assumed she was trans.

"Detective, have a seat. Our group was so upset to hear about Kevin's murder. We're planning a memorial at the Center for him. Such a lovely, kind man."

"We're trying our best to solve this," Brenda said. "I was hoping you could help. Are you a psychologist or other mental health professional?"

"Are you asking if I'm bound by professional confidentiality rules? The answer is not really. I'm more of a mentor. I've been trans for a long time and live a happy life. I try to make it easy for newer trans people to share their struggles. We do have a confidentiality pledge in our group. What is confided within the group stays there, but murder is an exception.

"I didn't hear about Kevin's death until Wednesday. I called our group members and we met yesterday. I'll share what I know about Kevin, and this is with the knowledge and consent of the rest of our group members. We want his murder solved. If you hadn't called me this morning, I was going to phone the police."

Brenda breathed a sigh of relief. Cooperative witnesses were a blessing. "What can you tell me about Kevin's life that might have put him at risk? Did he have any enemies?

Can you think of any motive other than hate for his murder?"

Esther sat back in her chair, hands clasped tightly together. "When Kevin first came to Hollywood, like many women who wanted to transition, he had no money and no job. He was homeless and worked as a female prostitute on Santa Monica Boulevard. That was about fifteen years ago."

Brenda remembered being a rookie and seeing the trans women waiting for johns when she made her patrol rounds.

Esther took a breath and continued. "Then he discovered the LGBT Center and began to take hormones and transition. He took any menial job he could find, and finally ended up getting MediCal and disability payments. They weren't enough to support him, but he was able to rent a cheap apartment. Unfortunately, he still needed money to live on and couldn't find a regular job, so he continued to work as a male prostitute."

"Being a trans prostitute is particularly dangerous," Brenda said. "When I was assigned to Hollywood station, we got lots of assaults, particularly on trans women, but trans men weren't exempt. The kind of men, gay or straight, who pick up a male prostitute can get pretty angry when they discover they haven't gotten what they paid for."

Esther ran her hands through her long hair. "Kevin figured that out pretty quickly, after a few beatings. He told potential clients he was trans up front. This decreased his income, but was somewhat safer. There are men, both gay and straight, who are turned on by the thought of sex with a trans prostitute. Kevin caught a few STDs but, for a while, didn't get beaten."

That information was consistent with what Brenda had learned from Hannah.

"Did anything change recently?"

"Yes. He met Dolly. I'd never seen him so happy. He didn't want to give her an STD so he stopped selling himself. A few weeks ago, he said he wanted to buy her a ring."

Brenda hadn't noticed a ring on Dolly's finger, and she hadn't said anything about a more permanent commitment.

"Let me guess. He didn't have the money."

"Right. He decided to get it the fastest way he knew, so he went back on the street."

Brenda suspected that decision had been a mistake. Esther appeared increasingly agitated, tapping her foot and staring at the floor.

"Did he say anything about what happened? Anything that could have led to his murder?"

Esther waited before answering, finally raising her head to meet Brenda's gaze.

"He told the group that most of the guys on the street were one or two decades younger than he was, and he had trouble attracting johns. No one wants a hooker over forty. He was going to try one more time, and if he didn't make any money, he'd give it up. That was the last time he came to our group. We meet every Monday night." Her eyes began to water. "We were told he'd died the following Sunday."

"I'm sorry. You've been a real help. One more question. Do you know exactly where Kevin hung out to be picked up?"

"Santa Monica, near Highland."

"Looks like I have my work cut out for me," Brenda said. "Thanks so much. I can't talk about an active case, but I promise to let you know when we solve it."

CHAPTER SEVENTEEN

W HEN BRENDA EMERGED FROM THE CENTER, Daniel was leaning on the black-and-white.

"Any luck?" she asked.

"Nothing new. Ryan was upset at Kevin's death. Everyone seems to have liked him, but didn't know anything about his personal life. Doctor Ryan just supplied the hormones. Kevin never had the financial resources for any surgery. How about you? Learn anything?"

Brenda slid into the passenger seat. "Quite a bit. Let's head back and I'll fill you in."

As they drove, Brenda briefed Daniel. "I guess my next step is trying to interview some of the male prostitutes on the boulevard."

"Take someone with you, please," Daniel said. "I'd go, but that would be giving Hannah a motive for murder."

"Not to worry. Enjoy your vacation. I'll take one of the rookies." She grinned at him. "Are you ready to spend some real time with your son?"

"Honestly, I'm a little nervous. I have no idea what to expect from a thirteen-year-old boy."

"You were thirteen once. What's the worst thing you ever did?"

Daniel laughed. "I stole my father's brand new Mercedes convertible and took it on a joy ride. He went ballistic and grounded me for a month."

"Did you damage it?"

"Of course not. I don't think I exceeded ten miles an hour. I'd never driven before. My father got even by stopping me from getting a learner's permit until I was sixteen."

"I strongly suggest you keep the keys to your vintage Mustang on you at all times," Brenda said. "I can't wait to hear everything when you get back from your week off."

"Wish me luck," Daniel said.

Brenda was off for the weekend, but she decided she shouldn't miss the opportunity to interview the male prostitutes on Saturday night. The largest number would be there, and perhaps one of them might know Kevin, or have seen who picked him up. She also thought there might be some security footage that could be helpful.

When she got back to the station, she checked the call schedule to see which teams were on Saturday night and noticed Alberto Figueroa, the rookie who'd found Kevin's body, was assigned to work. She'd had a good impression of him and was relieved it wasn't Henderson. After his transphobic comment, he wasn't exactly on her A list.

She printed out a few photos of Kevin and gave Alberto a call.

"Alberto, it's detective Jordan. We may have a lead on the Kevin Chase murder. Can you come to Hollywood with me tomorrow night and interview some prostitutes?"

"Sure. What time should I meet you?"

He actually sounded excited. Ah, to be a newbie again and be thrilled to chase down a murder suspect.

"I'll meet you here about ten p.m. We'll take an unmarked car so they won't scatter when we pull up. Wear civilian clothes."

"You got it, detective. See you tomorrow."

Brenda hung up the phone, grabbed her purse and headed out to her car. She was looking forward to a leisurely dinner out with Marcy and sleeping in on Saturday morning.

When Brenda got home, she found Marcy sprawled on the sofa. An open bottle of Pinot Noir and two wine glasses were set out on the coffee table.

"What's the occasion?" Brenda removed her jacket, put her gun in the safe, and walked over to plant a kiss on Marcy's forehead. "A glass of good wine is just what I need."

"It's Friday night. I made dinner reservations at one of your favorite Italian restaurants, and you've got the weekend off. What more of an occasion do we need?"

Marcy poured two glasses of wine. Brenda accepted hers and sat on the sofa. They clinked glasses. It wasn't exactly a whole weekend off, but Brenda didn't think she needed to mention that just yet.

"To being ourselves and to hell with everyone else," Marcy toasted.

"I'll second that."

"I've been doing a lot of thinking since dinner at the Cheesecake Factory. There's something I'd like to ask you." Marcy put her wine glass back on the table. "Since you came into my life, I'm happier than I've ever been. Will you marry me?"

Tears welled in Brenda's eyes. She'd thought about marriage the day California made it legal in June of 2013, but she'd been afraid to ask. She'd also wondered if it made any sense to be married in California and not married when they crossed the state line.

All her LGBT friends were following the case of Obergefell vs. Hodges as it wended its way through the Federal court system to the Supreme Court, but there was no guarantee that the court would do the right thing. To be totally honest, she also knew that marriage meant coming out of the closet, and she hadn't been ready then. She was ready now.

"Of course I will." Brenda leaned in for a long kiss.

"At some point, you will need to invite your parents to the wedding," Marcy said, as they came up for air. "I wasn't sure you were ready until last week."

"Last week was an epiphany. I'll even tell people at work I'm engaged, and if I get any homophobic flack I'll report it to human resources. I'm ready to open the closet door."

"I'll drink to that. My plan for the weekend is dinner at Pizzicotto tonight, and tomorrow we can go shopping for engagement rings. I saw some beautiful ones in a jewelry store in Santa Monica, on Montana."

"And, we can start thinking about planning a wedding," Brenda said. "I'd like it small, intimate and sooner, rather than later."

After a dinner of pasta and tiramisu, followed by a night of lovemaking, Brenda awoke from the most relaxing sleep she could remember. Marcy was still breathing gently in a fetal position.

Brenda tiptoed to the bathroom, and then to the kitchen, closing the bedroom door behind her. She brewed a big pot of coffee and made some batter for blueberry pancakes, Marcy's favorite. Happiness bubbled up inside her like a whistling tea kettle. She was engaged to the love of her life. She never thought this could happen to her.

The sound of the shower alerted her that Marcy was up and she began heating the grill and setting the table for breakfast. When Marcy, wrapped in her favorite terry robe, entered the kitchen, Brenda handed her a steaming mug.

"How many blueberry pancakes would you like?" she asked.

"If I'd known you were going to cook me pancakes, I'd have proposed months ago. Two please."

Brenda poured two scoops of batter for Marcy and two more for herself. There were few things as relaxing as a weekend breakfast.

"Ready to go ring shopping today?" Marcy asked.

"Can't wait."

"I was thinking we could take in a movie tonight. There are several good ones playing in the neighborhood."

"I can't, babe." Brenda sighed. "I didn't mention it yesterday, but I have a tiny bit of work I have to do late Saturday night."

"You're going to work on your weekend off, on our engagement weekend!"

"I didn't know it was going to be our engagement weekend. Unfortunately, the witnesses I need to talk to will only be available tonight."

"Is this the hate crime case again? What witnesses can't

wait until Monday? Are you ever going to put us ahead of solving your crimes?"

"Don't be angry. I got a good lead yesterday and I want to interview as many male prostitutes as possible on Santa Monica Boulevard tonight. I'm hoping one or more of them can help me identify the guys responsible for killing Kevin Chase."

She flipped the pancakes over, waited a minute and loaded them onto their plates. She handed one to Marcy and sat down. Marcy ignored it.

"So you're going to a dangerous neighborhood to talk to some guy whores, late at night. Did it occur to you that you could get hurt?"

Brenda poured some maple syrup on her pancakes and took a breath. She needed to defuse this. The last thing she wanted was a fight.

"I know you worry about me, but please don't. I'm taking a big, six-foot tall cop with me and we'll both be armed. We'll just talk to them and offer to pay them for useful information. I won't get hurt."

Marcy said nothing, but she took a bite of the pancakes and sipped her coffee.

"Maybe I wasn't clear about how much solving this crime means to me," Brenda said. "An LGBT hate crime affects all of us. It's an attack on our community and I take it personally. Otherwise I wouldn't be working on my weekend off."

"What about Daniel?"

"Daniel's on vacation for a week. I'm on my own and I want to prove myself, not just to him, but to me. I need to know I'm ready to take the lead now."

Marcy sighed. "Okay, but don't make a habit of it. Weekends off are special."

"I'll protect them as much as I can," Brenda promised.

She reached across the table and took Marcy's hand. "What kind of a stone would you like in your engagement ring?"

CHAPTER EIGHTEEN

HANNAH AWOKE WITH A KNOT IN THE PIT OF HER stomach. Today was the day that might change all their family dynamics. She was totally unprepared for the addition of a thirteen-year-old boy of unknown temperament. She'd forgiven Daniel for the one-night-stand that had produced Josh, and almost destroyed their marriage before it began. Still, the shock, to both of them, of discovering Josh on their honeymoon, lingered.

She rolled over in bed and saw that Daniel's side was empty. The smell of coffee was wafting in from the kitchen. Dragging herself up, she brushed her teeth, and stood for a long time in an extra hot shower, shampooing her long red hair. She combed it out, pulled the wet mass into a ponytail, and dressed in jeans and a black turtleneck sweater.

Daniel and Zoe were in the midst of breakfast.

Zoe saw her, abandoned her cereal and ran to her for a hug. "Mommy, I'm so excited. I can't wait."

Hannah held her tightly. "I know you are." *Why couldn't she be?*

Hannah glanced over at Daniel, seeing the anxiety in his eyes. "Did Josh's flight from Bellingham take off on time?"

"He's scheduled to land at one p.m. at LAX," he said. "Zoe and I will leave early so we have plenty of time to get a gate pass and meet him. He's traveling as an unaccompanied minor."

Hannah planted a kiss on Zoe's forehead and delivered her back to her dining chair. Then she poured herself a mug of coffee. She felt too tense to eat anything, and the caffeine probably wasn't a great idea either.

"Nervous?" she asked, as she took her place at the table.

"A little. I keep reminding myself that Josh is going to be nervous too. He's meeting a father he didn't know existed, a stepsister and a stepmother. I'd be scared in his place."

Hannah recognized a plea when she heard one. "Don't worry. We'll give him a warm welcome. Zoe and Emilia even baked a chocolate welcome cake for him yesterday."

"With frosting?" Daniel asked.

Zoe's smile lit up the room. "Chocolate frosting, and it says *Welcome, Josh* in vanilla."

"He's going to love it, sweetie," Hannah said.

"Can we have pizza for dinner?" Zoe asked.

Hannah had been debating what to make for dinner. How do you feed a kid who is used to meals from a five star chef?

"What do you think?" she asked Daniel.

"I think we should ask him what his favorite foods are and go from there. As I recall, my palate wasn't that sophisticated at thirteen. All those five star meals might have been lost on him. Maybe he's a kid who'd be thrilled to eat at McDonald's."

"God forbid," Hannah said. "CPK for pizza, yes. Fast food, absolutely not."

Daniel rose from the table and slipped his arms around her. "You're the boss."

Hannah didn't feel like the boss. If she was really in control, she might have had the courage to tell Daniel that she wasn't ready for Josh. It had barely been five months since she'd miscarried their baby, and another woman's teenaged son wasn't her idea of how to expand their family.

How could she even think about getting pregnant again when she had no idea of how much of their time and energy Josh might require? What if she didn't like him? What kind of damage would that do to her new marriage?

Daniel sat at the Alaska gate with Zoe, checking his watch every few minutes.

"Daddy, they're coming." Zoe got up, and Daniel stood as the first travelers disembarked from Josh's flight.

"It'll be a little while. He'll be escorted by a flight attendant who has to make sure he meets the right adult."

Ten minutes later, Daniel recognized the skinny figure in jeans and a T-shirt with the shock of black hair, like his own. Josh was carrying a large backpack. Daniel waved. He didn't remember Josh being so tall. He must have had a growth spurt in the six months since Daniel had last seen him.

"Is this your father?" the flight attendant asked.

Josh nodded. Daniel walked towards him, smiling, feeling the tension in his body and the tears that he forced back. This had to be even harder for Josh than it was for him.

"May I see some ID, sir?"

Daniel pulled out his driver's license and she photographed it with her phone.

"Thank you. Can't be too careful. You have a great time, Josh."

As she walked away, Daniel debated whether to greet his son with a hug or a handshake. Zoe, usually so shy with strangers, preempted him.

She ran over and reached out both arms. "I'm your sister, Zoe. Welcome to LA."

Josh grinned, squatted down to her level, (not an easy task given the weight of his backpack), and gave her a hug.

Daniel extended a hand to help him up. "We're all very happy to have you here. Do you have any more luggage at baggage claim?"

"Just my pack."

"Okay, let's head to the car." Daniel led the way to the LAX parking garage.

"OMG, is that a 1965 Mustang?" Josh asked, as Daniel put the backpack in the trunk. "I love old cars."

"Me too," Daniel said. "I put a lot of work into getting this one up to speed."

As he inserted his keys into the driver's side door, he reminded himself not to throw them on the hall table when they got home.

CHAPTER NINETEEN

HANNAH WAS WAITING AT THE OPEN FRONT DOOR AS Daniel's car pulled up. She pasted a warm smile on her face and greeted Josh. This had better go smoothly.

"Come on in. I'm Hannah." She extended her hand, and Josh shook it.

Daniel unloaded the trunk. Josh grabbed his pack and followed Hannah inside.

"Are you guys hungry? I don't think Alaska Airlines serves meals on a two hour flight."

"I could use a snack," Josh said. "Milk and cookies?"

"Me too, Mommy."

"You got it. Let's show Josh his room first." Hannah led the way down the hall to the guest room.

It was a spacious room, with sliding glass doors that led to the back yard, a wall lined with teak shelves and drawers, and a built-in desk. Hannah had hung framed posters of photos taken by the Hubble telescope, and had purchased crisp new navy-blue linens for the bed.

"This will be your room, whenever you stay with us," she said. "I remembered you were an astronomy fan."

Josh dropped his pack on the floor, looked out at the view over the hills, and smiled at her. "It's cool. Thank you."

"My room is down the hall," Zoe said. "And I've got some good video games."

"That's great Zoe. Maybe we can play later."

"Let's take Josh to the kitchen," Hannah said.

So far, so good. He seemed like a nice kid, and the room had met with his approval. Her tension level subsided a bit.

Daniel was in the kitchen, already munching on an apple. Hannah brought out glasses, milk, and an assortment of cookie boxes. Everyone sat.

"I thought I'd ask you what your favorite foods are, Josh," she said, "so I'll know what to make for dinner."

"I'm easy. I like pretty much everything. Hamburgers, pizza, mac and cheese. Not a big fish fan. The restaurant made too many fish dishes."

"I don't like fish either," Zoe announced. "Except for tuna sandwiches."

"Great. How about we barbecue hamburgers tonight?"

"I'm on board," Daniel said. "So, buddy, do you have any ideas about what you'd like to do while you're here?"

Josh's face lit up. "Yeah. I'd love to see a Dodger game, visit the Griffith Park planetarium, go to the beach, and Disneyland, of course."

Of course, Hannah thought. There were few things as exhausting for adults as Disneyland.

Josh finished his snack and looked up at Daniel. "Any chance we could shoot some hoops?"

"Sure," Daniel said.

Hannah sensed Zoe wanting to join in and she deflected her. "How about you help me get stuff ready for dinner? I think Dad wants a chance to get to know Josh a little better."

Zoe nodded her assent. She looked disappointed, but Hannah knew she got it.

That night, Hannah served burgers, baked beans and coleslaw outside on the patio, and they watched as the lights went on over the city. She and Zoe cleared the table and brought in dessert.

"This is your welcome to the family cake," Zoe said. "I baked it."

"Wow, my Mom never mentioned I was going to have a kid sister who could bake."

Zoe's face lit up. Hannah cut and served, and everyone dug in.

When he was finished, Josh yawned. "I got up really early this morning. If you don't mind, I'm going to go to my room, unpack and crash."

"Good idea," Daniel said. "See you in the morning."

"I'm not tired, Mommy. Can I watch TV?"

"Sure," Hannah said. "Daniel and I will take care of the dishes, and then I'll read to you and tuck you in."

Hannah waited for the sound of the TV and turned to Daniel.

"So, how's it going?"

He shrugged. "So far, okay. I admit I'm feeling a little awkward."

"Me too. I guess we just have to take it one day at a time. He seems nice."

"His mother probably told him to be on his best behavior. Never underestimate a thirteen-year-old."

Hannah curled up on Zoe's bed next to her, and opened *Harry Potter and the Sorcerer's Stone*. Zoe leaned back on her shoulder and Hannah held her. This was her favorite time, their nightly snuggle. Zoe was now reading fluently, although when she was tired, she still preferred to close her eyes and listen.

"Chapter Four." Hannah began, reading in a soft voice. She felt Zoe relax and the rhythm of her breathing slowed.

As she finished the chapter, she lowered Zoe to her pillow and kissed her forehead. "Goodnight, sweetie."

"Mommy, what's that funny smell?"

Hannah took a deep breath and recognized the scent. Fury filled her.

"The neighbors must be cooking something weird," she said. "You go to sleep and I'll check it out."

She turned off the light, and closed Zoe's door behind her. Then she marched down the carpeted hall to Josh's room. As she got closer, the scent got stronger. She was positive now. Reaching for the doorknob, she paused. This wasn't her problem to solve. Disciplining Josh was on Daniel.

She turned around and headed for the den. Daniel was watching TV. She grabbed the control and turned it off.

"You need to have a talk with Josh, now. Your thirteen-year-old son is smoking marijuana in our house. You're the cop. Do something parental."

Daniel stood at Josh's door and took a deep breath. Hannah was right. His son was definitely smoking weed. It was so wrong on so many levels. He turned the knob.

Josh was out on the patio with the sliding glass doors

open. When he heard Daniel, he dropped his joint, crushed it under his foot, and turned to smile.

"We need to have a conversation," Daniel said.

Josh's eyebrows rose. "Is something wrong?"

"There are many things wrong. You haven't been here for twenty-four hours and you've broken two state and one federal law, and potentially gotten me in trouble."

"I'm sorry. Weed's legal in Washington."

"It's legal for adults, not for thirteen-year-olds. How did you get it?"

"My Mom uses it occasionally to relax. I took some of hers."

"Does she know you smoke?"

Josh shook his head.

"So that's four laws. Stealing is also illegal. You took pot on a plane. You are so lucky that a police dog didn't find it. You'd have been in deep trouble. It's also illegal in California and you were smoking it at the home of a police officer. I don't want my seven-year-old daughter inhaling second-hand smoke."

"I'm really sorry. I won't do it again."

"No, you won't. Hand it over."

Josh went to his backpack and removed a plastic baggie full of weed. Daniel took the backpack and searched it thoroughly. Then he checked the dresser drawers, and all of the pockets in Josh's clothing. Finding nothing more, he pocketed the baggie and sat down on the bed.

"Are you going to tell my Mom?"

"Josh, there's a reason marijuana is only legal in Washington for adults. We don't know enough about its effects on the developing brain. You are very smart, and have the potential to do so many interesting things with your life. I don't want drug use to interfere with who you can become."

"If you're so concerned about my brain, why'd it take you thirteen years to come and see me?"

Daniel sighed and pushed back his hair with both hands. "I had no idea you even existed until six months ago. If I hadn't made a reservation at your Mom's B&B, I still wouldn't know."

"Why didn't she tell you when she got pregnant?"

"You'll have to ask her that question, but I can make some guesses. I only spent one night with your mother, and it was a few days before I was decommissioned and left Washington. She may not have known where to find me, or she may not have tried because she didn't want some guy, who was really a stranger, having a say in your life."

"What would you have done, if she'd told you? Would you have married her, and been my dad for real?"

"You do know how to ask the hard questions. We barely knew one another, so I don't think we would have gotten married, but I would have done then what I'm trying to do now, which is take some responsibility for you. I'd have helped support you, kept in touch, visited, and had you come here to spend time with me when you were old enough. I can't make it up to you for missing your childhood, but I'm hoping you can help me be the kind of dad you want to have."

Josh didn't say anything. He just paced around the bedroom, taking it in and avoiding Daniel's glance. Finally, he sat down.

"Can we forget about this and start over?"

Daniel put a hand on Josh's shoulder. "Sounds like a good idea to me."

Josh stared at him. "What do you want me to call you?"

"Whatever feels comfortable to you, Josh. Daniel is fine. Dad, when you feel ready."

"I'm tired, Daniel."

Daniel ruffled his hair. "Get some sleep. Maybe we'll go to the beach tomorrow."

~

Hannah looked up as Daniel entered the bedroom. "Problem dealt with?"

"After I pointed out that he'd broken state and federal laws, and confiscated his weed, he promised he wouldn't do it again." Daniel took the baggie out of his pocket and showed it to her.

"Won't do it here. How do you know he won't be using drugs at home? I hope you're planning to tell his mother."

"We had a really good talk, Hannah. If I tell his mother, he'll never trust me again," Daniel said.

"I see he knows how to play you. Did he make you feel guilty for not finding him sooner?"

Daniel didn't respond. That meant she'd guessed right. If it was up to her, Josh would be on a plane to Bellingham tomorrow. The last thing she needed was Zoe being exposed to drugs.

"Can we just get some sleep and talk about this in the morning?" Daniel said. "We've both had a stressful day."

Hannah got into bed, pulled up the quilt, and rolled over on her right side, her back facing him. She heard the sounds of Daniel undressing and pulling on his pajamas. Finally, the light went out. He slipped under the covers, and without touching her, began the deep slow breaths of sleep.

CHAPTER TWENTY

After a successful morning of shopping, Brenda and Marcy chose identical settings for their rings with different center stones. Brenda's was an aquamarine, to set off her blue eyes. Marcy chose a golden topaz, which went well with her dark brown hair. After a late afternoon movie and an early Thai dinner, Brenda prepared for her rendezvous with Hollywood hustlers.

Dressed in jeans, and a khaki windbreaker long enough to hide her holster, she picked up Alberto in front of the West LA Station Saturday night. He was also in jeans and a faded brown leather bomber jacket.

"Are you armed?" she asked as he slid into the passenger seat.

"Shoulder holster. Do I need to be?"

"Probably not, but I like to be prepared for anything."

At night, this was a rough neighborhood. Brenda wasn't one to reach for a gun lightly, and she hoped the rookie wouldn't get nervous and act without orders.

"Where are we headed?"

Brenda turned right on Santa Monica Boulevard. "We're going to Highland. I was told that our victim was hanging out there, trying to get picked up. I'm hoping one or more of the prostitutes saw the pickup and might have more information."

"So these are all gay guy hookers?" Alberto was looking a bit uncomfortable. She remembered how surprised he'd been when Kevin's body revealed him to be trans.

"They're not all gay. Many of them are homeless teenage runaways, who sell themselves to eat. There are also drug addicts. The johns are often middle-aged gays who are in the closet or in denial. If they pick the wrong prostitute they sometimes get more than they paid for. When I was working Hollywood there were plenty of muggings and stabbings, not to mention complaints from residents on the side streets about guys in cars, parked in front of their homes, 'doing it'."

"So are we under cover?"

"Sort of. They won't talk to us if they know we're cops. We'll make it clear we're willing to pay for relevant information. Hopefully they won't run when they see us. Just follow my lead."

"This is much more interesting than patrolling west LA. Thanks for asking me to come with you, ma'am."

"Please call me Brenda. Ma'am makes me feel ancient."

Brenda reached into her purse at the next red light and handed Alberto a bunch of photos of Kevin. "We'll talk to them together and see what we can learn."

There was no problem finding a parking spot on Santa Monica Boulevard. This stretch was commercially dead. There was a Mobil station on the south side of the street, and a brightly lit doughnut shop on the north side. The rest of the boulevard was dark, bleak and industrial with storage units and warehouses, a depressing contrast to the lively restaurant, gym and bar scene in West Hollywood.

Brenda and Alberto got out of the car and walked to the stretch of street where half a dozen young hustlers were lounging in doorways, leaning on cars or against walls. The scent of marijuana permeated the air. A skinny blonde guy with a scant beard and long shaggy hair approached them.

"You two looking for a threesome?"

"Actually," Brenda said, "we're looking for information and willing to pay for it."

The hooker gave her a suspicious look as she handed him a photo of Kevin.

"You know this guy?"

He glanced down. Brenda saw the flash of recognition. "Why?"

"He's disappeared. We're from the LGBT center. Kevin was one of our clients, and we found out he'd been here last weekend. We're trying to find out if a john picked him up."

Alberto glanced at her. She sensed his surprise at her approach, and some definite discomfort. Straight guys didn't do well, pretending to be gay.

"I remember him. He's a little old for this gig. Most of the johns prefer younger meat. I wasn't here last weekend, but maybe some of the other guys might know."

He let out a whistle and motioned for the others to come forward. Several guys strolled leisurely in their direction.

"The lady's paying for information. Any of you seen this guy last weekend?" He held out the photo, and Alberto passed out a few more.

A tall black teenager with gold hoops in his ears answered. "Yeah. The old guy. He was out of practice, but he finally got a coupla johns. Two white guys in a car."

"Those two are bad news," the blonde commented. "The rest of us avoid them."

"Bad news, why?" Brenda asked.

"Two on one is asking to get beat up. Eddie here learned that the hard way a few weeks ago." The blonde pointed to a skinny white kid with track marks on both lower arms and tattoos on his biceps.

"Can you tell me what happened, Eddie?" Brenda asked.

Eddie glanced at his fellows. Brenda sensed his unwillingness to tell his story in front of them.

"Guys, thanks for your help. We'd like to talk to Eddie in private." She passed out twenty dollar bills to the other three. She had mixed feelings about the fact that any money she gave them would probably be spent on drugs.

Eddie leaned on the nearest car. "These two guys told me to get into the back of their car."

"Can you describe them?" Alberto asked.

"They were white guys with very short blond hair. Didn't get a good look at their faces, cause I was in the back, and when we all got out, they'd put on ski masks. That creeped me out a little."

"Where did they take you?" Brenda asked.

"Not far. Some apartment building with an underground garage in Hollywood. Wasn't watching the street signs. I was high at the time."

Damn. A witness on drugs wouldn't be at all useful in court.

"What happened next?" Brenda asked.

"They took me upstairs to an apartment. It didn't look like anyone lived there. I saw a couch and TV in the living room, and the bedroom was outfitted like a dungeon."

"What do you mean, dungeon?" Alberto asked.

"You know. Kind of a gym for people into the BDSM

scene. There was a bed with railings, cuffs, collars, nipple rings, leather, whips, slings, even a cage. The first thing they did was gag me. Then they cuffed me to the bed and whipped the shit out of me."

"How did you escape?"

"They finished torturing me, paid me, stuck me back in the car, dumped me on Fountain, and let me go. I couldn't move for days. A buddy let me sleep it off at his crib. Good thing I had plenty of oxy."

"When you left the building, did you notice where you were and what it looked like?" Brenda asked.

"Shit, no. I was lying on the back seat. Couldn't see anything."

"What about the car? Did you notice the make or the color?"

"It was black. Looked new. Seat covers were fabric, not leather, kinda scratchy. Didn't notice the make. Looked ordinary."

Brenda had a final thought. "Eddie, if I have more questions, how can I reach you?"

"I gotta phone." Eddie reached into his jeans pocket and pulled out what looked like an old iPhone. Brenda wondered if he'd stolen it.

She removed two twenties from her jacket and handed them to him. "Thanks for the very useful information. You've helped a lot. I can give you more if you're willing to loan me your phone for a few days. I think the guy we're looking for may have wound up in that apartment, and maybe your phone can help me find the location."

Eddie's glance was a combination of greed and suspicion. "How do I know I can trust you to return it?"

"You don't. How much money would make it worth your while to take the risk that I'm honest?"

He thought about it. "A hundred."

Brenda wondered how much heroin that would buy. She took five twenties, most of her remaining funds, out of her jacket.

"I need to know when this happened," Brenda said. "And I need your last name. Can you look at your calendar with me?"

"Name's Williams. It was a Saturday night, three weeks ago."

"You sure?"

"Yeah. Took me two weeks to feel up to doing tricks again. This is my first Saturday back."

He handed the phone to Brenda, and she exchanged it for the cash.

"I'll return the phone Wednesday night. Eight p.m. I'll meet you in front of the doughnut shop."

Eddie stuffed the dollars in his front pocket and slouched away.

Alberto gave Brenda a high five. "Looks like we got a lead."

"I hope so. How about I treat you to coffee and a few doughnuts?"

Alberto held open the door of the doughnut shop and the two of them walked in. They smelled a lovely scent of cinnamon and coffee. The shop was small, with a few booths, most were filled with women chatting. The talk subsided as they entered and were assessed.

"Tell me your favorite doughnut flavors, and grab that empty booth. I'll get us coffee."

Alberto pointed out the jelly doughnuts and the chocolate ones, and slid into the booth. Brenda ordered two coffees and selected half a dozen doughnuts. She'd bring the extras home to Marcy, who had a weakness for them.

"Jordan, is that you, girl? I thought you'd been transferred out of Hollywood." A short, plump Latina, with long curly hair, wearing large red hoop earrings, walked over with a grin on her face.

"Maria! I'm glad to see you. I'm not stationed in Hollywood. I'm in West LA now."

"What'cha doin' here? And who's the guy?"

Brenda motioned her over. "This is Patrolman Figueroa. Alberto, meet Maria. I met her during my time at the Hollywood station."

"She forgot to say she saved my ass," Maria said. "Two guys were beating me up because I'm trans, and she and another cop arrested them. Then she drove me to the ER at Hollywood Presbyterian."

Alberto's eyes widened. Brenda guessed he hadn't realized Maria was trans. Two other women, who'd been in Maria's booth, wandered over to listen in on the conversation. One looked as if she were in her sixties and had transitioned late. Another was a six-foot tall, gorgeous black woman, and after a minute Brenda recognized Dolly Divine.

"Don't I know you?" Dolly said.

Brenda held out her hand to shake Dolly's. "You do. I interviewed you a few days ago about Kevin. I'm Detective Jordan."

"Jordan's in charge of finding the bastard who killed your man?" Maria said. "She's the best cop in LAPD, and one of the few who cares about trans people."

Maria turned to Brenda. "You here tracking down the killer?"

Brenda nodded.

"You know who?" Dolly asked.

"Not yet, but we got a lead tonight."

"Why here? Kevin wasn't hustling anymore. He did that when he was young and poor, but he's got disability money now."

Brenda sighed. She hated to be the bearer of this news, but she thought Dolly deserved to know.

"I found out that Kevin was planning to propose to you, and he needed money for a ring. He was doing the wrong thing for the right reason, and he was picked up by two men who may have been his killers."

Dolly's eyes filled with tears. "Shit, shit shit. I didn't need no ring. I would'a married him. The idiot."

Maria put her arm around her friend and urged her to sit down. Brenda handed her a napkin and she blew her nose.

The three women crowded into the booth across from Alberto and Brenda.

"Is there anything we can do to help?" Maria asked. "There are trans women who are hookers. Maybe some of them have encountered the same johns. I could spread the word and see if anyone knows anything. I owe you one."

"You don't owe me for doing my job, but your help would be great, Maria. We're looking for two white guys, with very short blond hair, who are into S & M, and have a private apartment stocked with sex toys. Let's trade phone numbers so you can reach me if you find out anything, but be discreet and careful. I don't want you to put yourself or your friends in danger."

"Not to worry. I'll call if I hear something useful."

Maria wrote her number on a napkin. Brenda did the same. Then Maria and her companions got up and walked out the door, turning onto Highland Ave.

Brenda and Alberto finished their coffee and returned to Brenda's car.

"Thanks for coming along," Brenda said.

"Thanks for asking me. Now what?"

"Now, I'm taking all of tomorrow off, and I will see you Monday morning."

CHAPTER TWENTY-ONE

Brenda woke to the enticing scent of coffee and cinnamon. She wrapped herself in a robe, brushed her teeth and hair, and followed the scent to the kitchen. Marcy was seated at the table, sipping coffee and viewing the news on her laptop. When she spotted Brenda, she stood up and poured her a cup.

"Morning, sleepyhead. Sit."

Brenda sat. "What is that amazing smell?"

Marcy opened the oven and removed a loaf of freshly baked cinnamon raison bread.

"OMG, if we weren't already engaged, I'd propose on the spot."

Marcy handed her a plate with two slices of warm bread, and a container of whipped butter and orange marmalade.

"So, did you meet any cute male prostitutes last night?"

Brenda grinned. "I did, and I got a great lead to the killers. I just have to figure out how to follow it."

"Are you going to tell me?"

Brenda hesitated. She knew she wasn't supposed to discuss an ongoing investigation, but the last thing she wanted to do was to upset Marcy in any way. This was their engagement weekend, after all.

"Confidentially, I found a witness who saw the victim being picked up by two white guys in a car. My witness had gone with them a few weeks previously, and they had taken him to an apartment in Hollywood, outfitted with equipment for bondage, discipline, and sadomasochism, BDSM for short. They tied him up, apparently hurt him pretty badly, and then let him go. The witness loaned me his phone so I could trace his movements, and possibly locate the apartment."

"That sounds like a big break. What's your next step?"

Brenda took another bite of the cinnamon bread and washed it down with the hot coffee.

"On Monday morning, I'll give the phone to Izzy and see if he can provide me with an address. If I can identify the actual apartment, I'll try to trace down the renters and get a search warrant. The other thing I want to try is to infiltrate the BDSM Hollywood community. I'm thinking these guys might show up at underground parties, and I might be able to identify them."

"Don't tell me you're going to a BDSM party all by yourself!"

Marcy did not look happy. Maybe telling her all this was a mistake.

"Not to worry. I'll bring along a partner. I'm getting fond of the rookie I worked with last night. He's got potential."

"What about Daniel?" Marcy asked. "Wouldn't you be better off with an experienced detective?"

"Daniel is taking a week off to bond with his newly discovered thirteen-year-old son. Hannah would never forgive me if I distracted him."

"Do you know anything about BDSM?" Marcy asked.

Brenda laughed. "I learned a little when I was stationed in Hollywood, enough to know it's not considered a sex crime. BDSM is a community of people with a sexual preference that is practiced with consent. The large parties are a way of providing protection so that participants are not abused."

"Your description of what happened to that prostitute sounds like he was abused."

Brenda got up and poured herself a second mug of coffee. "Exactly. These guys were off the grid. It's possible to establish and insist on rules of conduct at a club or a private party, but in the privacy of your apartment, you can do anything, especially if you've picked up a prostitute."

"Sounds creepy to me," Marcy said. "So do you have to dress in black leather to go to one of these parties?"

"I can't afford leather," Brenda said. "Anyway, the leather scene is mostly gay men. I'm betting that these killers might show up at some big BDSM events. All I need to do is figure out where and when such events might take place."

Marcy slid the loaf of cinnamon bread in Brenda's direction. "That sounds like a perfect project for Monday. If you promise not to talk about it any more today, I'll loan you my leather jacket."

The first thing Brenda did upon arrival at the station Monday morning was to brief Izzy on her Saturday night experiences and hand over the evidence bag with the phone.

"I'll take this down to the lab and have them get prints before I work on your GPS coordinates. Never know when they might come in handy."

"Thanks Izzy. Let me know when you get something."

Returning to her desk, Brenda pulled up a list of the current detectives in the Hollywood division. She had a feeling that their sex crimes detectives might be able to help. She was pleased to discover that Alicia Jenkins, an African American officer about ten years her senior, was now head detective in Sex Crimes.

There hadn't been many women in the Hollywood division when she'd started there, right out of the academy, and Alicia had been a savvy mentor. She had been kind, amusing, and had taught Brenda to take no shit from any of her fellow police officers.

She picked up the phone. "Alicia, it's Brenda Jordan. I'm in West LA Division, homicide, working a hate crime. Can I pick your brain?"

"Most of my brain feels like mush this morning, girl, but you're welcome to what's left."

Brenda briefed her on the Kevin Chase murder and the two guys she was looking for. "So, how would you advise me to infiltrate the BDSM scene?"

"Gay or straight scene?" Alicia asked.

"Are they separate?"

"The straight parties are happy to host anyone who wants to play, but there are groups that are exclusively gay male or lesbian. From your description of the victims, I'd bet your suspects are straight, homophobic, racist, transphobic white men."

"I think so too. Are there places close to Hollywood that they might go to?"

"The way this works is that there are a number of large event spaces called dungeons. They are usually stocked with all kinds of kinky equipment and often have fantasy rooms for play-acting scenes. The owner is usually a dominatrix, who rents the place out for events, and provides staff to help clients get the experience they want in a safe, non-judgmental way. I've gotten to know several of them because occasionally, but not often, things get out of hand and they call us."

Brenda ran her hands through her hair, imagining herself in a dungeon, wearing thigh high boots and a leather bustier, pretending to dominate a client. This undercover job was going to be harder than she thought.

"I have a suggestion," Alicia said. "I know a dominatrix named Mistress Lily. She owns a cool space and knows the scene. Why don't I give her a call and ask her to talk to you. Different dungeons attract different groups of clients. She would know where you would be most likely to find the guys you're looking for, provided they go to clubs. She even gives classes, training women who want to be dominatrixes."

"Just what I need," Brenda said. "People already complain I'm too bossy."

"A perfect fit, then," Alicia said. "You already know how to use cuffs."

Brenda laughed loudly, and several detectives looked in her direction to see what was so funny.

"I appreciate the contact," Brenda said. "You're the best. Let me know when Mistress Lily is available."

CHAPTER TWENTY-TWO

MISTRESS LILY HAD FREE TIME IN THE LATE afternoon and agreed to a meeting. Her event space was at the eastern end of West Hollywood, on the second floor of a 1920's Spanish Revival building. It was called *...And Dragons.*

Brenda had a mental image of the dominatrix. She would be six feet tall, wearing sheer black tights and thigh high boots with stiletto heels. Her curvaceous body would be sheathed in black leather and she would be wearing dark red lipstick.

The woman who greeted her at the door couldn't have been more of a surprise. Mistress Lily looked like a teenager, although she must have been at least in her thirties to own such a business. She was short and slim, wearing an LA Dodgers sweatshirt, jeans and Nikes. Pale blonde hair was pulled back into a ponytail and her face, with its pert nose and a sprinkling of freckles, was devoid of makeup.

She held out her hand and shook Brenda's. "Welcome, Detective. You chose the perfect day. Mondays are slow around here, after the weekend. We use Monday nights for our educational sessions. How can I help you?"

"I'm trying to solve a murder. My investigation so far has led to two white men who pick up male prostitutes and take them to a private space in Hollywood that has BDSM equipment. I thought these men might perhaps also frequent private parties at Dungeon spaces. Detective Jenkins from Hollywood division said you were familiar with the BDSM scene and might suggest places and events I could investigate further. Also, I don't know much about the BDSM scene, so I could use some general information."

Lily nodded. "Why don't we start with a tour of the premises so you can get a better idea of what goes on here."

She ushered Brenda into a large room. "This is our general meeting space. We use it for parties and our educational efforts. My Dungeon caters to beginners, people who are intrigued but need to know more."

The space was decorated in Victorian bordello style. There was burgundy flocked wallpaper, and red velvet loveseats and settees set against the wall. The center of the room had rows of chairs, facing a stage bordered with red satin fringed curtains.

"Down that hall, we have private rooms, designed for different kinds of fantasy play," Lily continued.

Brenda followed her as she opened door after door. There was a schoolroom with a teacher's desk, a blackboard and a student desk. Hooks on the wall held long rulers, whips, and a nun's costume.

The next room was medical. Its props included a gynecologic table with stirrups, a side table with surgical equipment, a stethoscope and metal cuffs.

The one that followed was a literal medieval dungeon with chains, a modified rack, and a metal cage, too small for standing up or lying down.

Brenda felt her anxiety level rising. This was beginning to creep her out. Did people actually enjoy this?

"Quite a setup," Brenda said.

"BDSM is about fantasy play. People can act out whatever roles turn them on, whether they wish to dominate or submit. I have a staff of men and women who serve as either tops or bottoms, depending on the client's desires. Couples also come here to play because they don't have the settings or equipment at home," Lily said.

"Tops?"

"A top dominates. A bottom submits," Lily explained.

"Are there rules about what people are permitted to do here?"

"We don't police activities between consenting adults. When my staff is involved, the bottoms have a safe word, and the absolute rule is that once the safe word is spoken, the activity stops. If a couple is using the room without my staff, the same rule applies. We haven't had any instances of people getting badly hurt during their activities, although there are some dungeons where that has happened."

The two of them returned to the main hall. "Why don't you come tonight to our educational session?" Lily suggested. "It's at seven o'clock. You could grab something to eat in the neighborhood, and we serve coffee and fabulous brownies at the event."

"I'll give my fiancé a call and tell her I won't make it home for dinner," Brenda said.

"She's welcome to come as well," Lily said.

"Thanks, but I don't mix my job with my private life."

"Have a seat," Lily motioned Brenda to one of the loveseats, and pulled up a chair for herself. "You wanted to know about some of the other dungeons in town."

"Are there some that would particularly appeal to the kind of men I described?"

"There's one I can think of in Hollywood. It caters to both straight and gay clients and there have been several incidents over the years where the owner had to call the police. If your guys get their kicks out of playing really rough, this would be the place. It's called *Kings of Dominion*. I can give you the contact information for the owner."

On her way out, Brenda phoned Marcy.

"I'm not going to make it home for dinner, babe."

"What's up?"

"I'm investigating what happens in dungeons, and the owner I interviewed invited me to come back at seven for one of their public educational sessions."

"Sounds like fun. Can I come?"

"Seriously? You want to visit a BDSM dungeon?"

"Why not? I bet Daniel would let Hannah come with him. It's not like I'd be in danger."

Damn. Brenda should have anticipated this. She didn't want Marcy there. What if Marcy wound up wanting to add a little B&D to their sex life? On the other hand, she didn't want to make Marcy angry. Giving in might be a smarter move.

"Just so you understand, Daniel never deliberately puts Hannah in a situation where she could be in danger. Hannah does that all on her own. Having said that, you're right. This isn't a dangerous situation. Can you meet me for dinner at six? I noticed a Thai place not far from here."

"It's a date," Marcy said. "I'll wear leather."

Brenda and Marcy returned to *...And Dragons* at 7:15 p.m. True to her word, Marcy was wearing her blue leather jacket, black suede slacks and knee-high boots. She looked hot.

The back of the hall was filled with people munching on brownies and cookies, and drinking coffee. The crowd looked as kinky as a PTA meeting. They ranged from middle-aged men and women in their Monday work suits, to young couples in their twenties. A few of the middle-aged men were engaged in enthusiastic conversation with much younger women who, Brenda suspected, were staff. There was a paucity of tattoos, bizarre haircuts or piercings. Not quite what she had expected.

Mistress Lily, in a chic, short black dress, with her blonde hair down, came out on the stage and asked for the crowd's attention.

"Please take your seats, ladies and gentlemen. We are about to begin our educational session. Welcome to those of you who are new. The subject of tonight's talk will be *Staying Safe in the Dungeon*. Let me introduce you to Mistress Judy and Mistress Lizzie."

Judy was a gorgeous black woman with Ethiopian features and a close-cut afro. She carried a large jar filled with brightly colored paper packages. Lizzie was a redhead, wearing cinnamon-colored leather pants and a matching jacket.

"Nice outfit," Marcy whispered.

Marcy and Brenda took seats in the back row, so Brenda could watch the crowd as well as the presentation. Marcy reached in back of Brenda and snagged a supply of brownies to share.

"Greetings," Judy said. "We're so happy you could join us. For those who haven't been here before, and I do see many new faces, know that BDSM is all about living your fantasies, safely and consensually, with your honey or with some irresistible new hottie. The first thing you need to be safe is one of these."

She opened the jar and passed a bright red square to Lizzie, who opened it and pulled out a condom.

"These come in all varieties. We have them with fruit-flavored lube, glow in the dark, your favorite colors and some nice ticklers at the end. The jar is at the entrance to the party room and guests are welcome to help themselves."

"Now," Judy continued. "You ladies may have encountered gentlemen who are reluctant to use them. 'They don't fit me. I'm just too big'."

There was laughter among the women.

Marcy squeezed Brenda's hand. "This session is a little on the straight side."

Lizzie was busy blowing up the condom she had unwrapped. It got bigger, and bigger, and BIGGER until it resembled the body of a Dachshund.

"If you know a guy who can't fit into this," Lizzie said, "send him my way."

The audience howled. Brenda and Marcy slipped out the door.

~

"Is there a dungeon for lesbians?" Marcy asked as they reached her car.

"I have no idea," Brenda said. "Why are you asking?"

"Just curious. Wondering what they give out to spice things up, instead of condoms."

"If I was the mistress, it would be chocolate," Brenda said, "and I just happen to have a box of chocolate truffles for you at home."

Marcy grinned. "You better hurry to your car. If I get home first, I might just finish them before you get there."

CHAPTER TWENTY-THREE

"Here's the phone back," Izzy said, handing Brenda a sealed plastic evidence bag the next morning. "And here's the address you were looking for, contact information for the building manager, and a tenant list. There are twenty units in the building."

"You are the best," Brenda said. "I don't know what this department would do without you."

"You still have to figure out which apartment it is before you can get a search warrant."

"No problem. At least now I know how to get started."

Brenda was not a fan of doing computer scut work when she could be out investigating in person, so she checked the schedule to see which newbies might be available to help. Morales was off today, but McCall and Henderson, the two rookies who'd helped interview at the homeless camp were available, so Brenda phoned and asked both of them to stop by her desk.

"I've got some work for the two of you. I need you to investigate the tenants at this address. One of these apartments is likely to be the crime scene for the murder I'm working on, only I have to identify it before any judge will give me a warrant. Use the most recent census, and any other database you can, to find out about the tenants who live in each unit."

"Exactly what are we looking for?" McCall asked, his lips pursing. He didn't look happy.

"I'm looking for a unit that is either occupied by one or two young white guys, or is a short term rental, the sort of place that might be rented by an out of town owner."

"So if a unit is lived in by a family, an elderly couple, or a black tenant, we can probably eliminate it?" Henderson asked.

"Right. One of those apartments is outfitted with equipment that is used for BDSM," Brenda said. "That's the one I need to search."

"How do you know that?" Henderson asked.

"I'm a very good detective," Brenda said. "You can grab any of the empty desks and log into the computer. I'll check back with you later this afternoon, or if you think you've got it, I'll be on my cell. I have a meeting later this morning."

As Brenda walked out of the detective pod, she overheard McCall say. "She sure is wasting a lot of time on that trans murder."

"No great loss, if you ask me," Henderson replied.

Brenda restrained herself from turning around and yelling, as she'd wanted to do during dinner with her father. It wouldn't change anything and she needed the extra hands. How many other of her police colleagues were transphobic or homophobic? It wouldn't take long to find out, once she announced her engagement to Marcy.

Thanks to the contacts of Mistress Lily, Brenda had a date to meet the owner of *Kings of Dominion* for a late breakfast at Canter's. The owner's name was Mistress Rose.

When Brenda arrived, the restaurant was relatively empty, in its weekday pause between breakfast and lunch. The scent of bakery products and corned beef permeated the air. An elderly lady with a cap of white hair, cut in a straight bob, a pair of wire-rimmed glasses, and a rosy complexion was seated at the entryway, reading this morning's LA Times. Brenda walked past the bakery to the restaurant entry and approached the maître d'.

"Table for one?" he asked.

"Actually I'm meeting someone. Her name is Rose."

"She's over there," he said, pointing behind Brenda. "I'll get you a booth."

The elderly lady stood up. She was wearing a gray turtleneck sweater with matching slacks and orthopedic shoes. She walked toward Brenda, limping slightly, and carrying a cane. The two of them were escorted to a booth in the back.

"Not what you expected, Detective?" Rose asked. She spoke with a New York accent. "You didn't think a nice Jewish grandmother would own a dungeon?"

"I'm learning that mistresses come in all shapes, sizes, races, and ages," Brenda said.

Rose laughed. "Actually it's been a family business since my parents started it in the thirties. My brothers managed it for some time, but after Morty passed away, and Herman developed Alzheimer's, I had to take over. My kids aren't interested in the business, so I'm trying to sell it."

The waiter arrived, and they paused to order bagels and

lox for Rose, and a Denver omelet for Brenda. He poured coffee for both of them.

"I do love this place," Brenda said. "In my line of work, I don't get to go out for breakfast very often."

Rose nodded. "How can I help you, Detective?"

"I'm looking for two white guys who look like neo-Nazis and who are into BDSM. They have a private apartment dungeon, where I believe they murdered someone and dumped the body in a homeless camp. Lily thought your club might be a place they would go to party. Does that description ring a bell?"

Rose took a bite of her bagel and chewed for awhile. "Unfortunately that description fits quite a few of our clients. It's a much rougher crowd than my parents catered to, at the beginning. The crowd is overwhelmingly male, both gay and straight, and they like giving and receiving a level of pain that most people can't tolerate."

"How do you keep your staff safe?" Brenda asked.

"My mistresses only act as tops, never bottoms, and I have well-trained security."

"When is your next event?" Brenda asked.

"Friday night."

"I'd like to go undercover and look around," Brenda said.

Rose laughed. "The only way you could do that is if you went as one of my mistresses. You know how to wield a whip?"

"I know how to take down a guy and put on handcuffs," Brenda said.

"Perfect. Be there at eight o'clock and I'll find you a costume."

"I could show up in full swat gear. More comfortable than one of those bustiers, and certainly dominating."

"You get points for originality, but I wouldn't want to risk anyone thinking you were for real. I've got lots of outfits that won't show your bubbies."

On her way out, Brenda stopped at the bakery to stock up on Danish pastry and black-and-white cookies. Since she was close to Hollywood, it wouldn't hurt to interview the building manager while she was awaiting data from her rookies.

As she was searching for her credit card, a childish voice called her name. She looked up and saw Daniel, Hannah, Zoe, and a tall teenager, who had to be Josh.

Zoe ran over to her for a hug.

"What are you guys doing here, Pumpkin?"

"We just went to the auto museum," Zoe announced. "I want a Ferrari when I grow up."

"Josh," Daniel said. "This is Detective Brenda Jordan, my partner. Brenda, this is my son, Josh."

Brenda held out her hand, and Josh shook it. She could see Daniel in the shape of Josh's face and his dark blue eyes. He'd be a heartthrob when he grew up and lost the pimples.

"I've heard lots about you. I hope you're enjoying LA."

"It's great so far."

Brenda glanced over at Hannah in time to catch an eye roll.

"We're introducing Josh to some ethnic food he can't get on the island," Hannah said.

"I recommend the corned beef sandwich," Brenda suggested. "It's to die for."

"You guys grab a booth," Daniel said. "I want to talk to Brenda for few minutes."

"So, how's the case doing?" Daniel asked.

"You first. How's fatherhood treating you?"

"It's a challenge. I wish we had more time to talk. There was a little incident with pot on his first night here."

The counterman handed Brenda her bag, and she offered Daniel a cookie. He shook his head.

"Okay, you can give me the details on Monday. Any other surprises?"

Daniel sighed. "We went to Zuma beach on Sunday and Josh couldn't stop talking about the hot girls in bikinis. They must not have them in the Northwest. I don't remember being so obsessed with girls at that age. Zoe couldn't understand why he seemed so interested in other girls, when she's a girl, and she was right there to build a sandcastle with him."

Brenda laughed. "Are he and Zoe getting along?"

"He has been sweet to her, but it's constant video games. I'm not sure if he lets her win or if she really is better at it than he is."

"She's a pretty smart kid. I'm glad she likes having a big brother. Is Hannah adjusting?"

"Hard to say. She was furious about the marijuana, but Josh was very apologetic the next morning. He's been asking her lots of questions about medicine, and they've had some good conversations, but it doesn't help that he's a slob. I told her not to look in his room."

"It's just a first visit. Give the kid a break. He's probably pretty nervous."

Brenda guided Daniel away from the counter, which was getting crowded with customers.

"Your turn. How is the case coming?" Daniel asked.

"I'm making progress. I'll brief you when you come back to work. I do miss you. If you weren't on vacation, you could be my date Friday night. I'm going undercover to a BDSM party, disguised as a mistress."

Daniel's eyebrows rose. "Seriously? I don't have to tell you to be careful."

"No, you don't. One more thing. I want you and Hannah to be the first to know. I did it. I proposed, Marcy accepted and we're engaged." She held out her left hand so Daniel could see her ring.

He reached out and drew her into a big hug. "I'm so happy for both of you. Have you told your parents?"

"Not yet." Her stomach knotted at the thought. "On my schedule when this case is solved. Gotta go, now. I'm on a hunt for a private dungeon in Hollywood."

A waiter escorted Hannah and the kids to a spacious booth in the back and took their orders. Zoe selected blueberry blintzes, Josh agreed to try the corned beef on rye, and Hannah ordered one for herself and Daniel's favorite, pastrami.

The waiter brought their drink orders and some pickles and sauerkraut.

Hannah sat back and tried to relax. The Auto Museum had been the first place Josh seemed genuinely interested in. She could see he was getting bored with all this family stuff.

Their meals arrived, and so did Daniel. Josh put some mustard and coleslaw on his sandwich and took a big bite. After swallowing, he grinned at them.

"This is so much better than those fancy foodie meals at my Mom's B&B," Josh said.

"Do you eat there every day?" Daniel asked.

"Hell, no. Just weekends. They serve things like fried oysters and kale quiches. During the week, it's Cheerios or Cocoa Puffs and milk at home for breakfast, and frozen food for dinners. The pizza's not bad. I bet if I had a kid sister, meals would be better." Josh reached over and pulled gently on Zoe's braid.

"I like having a big brother. Will you come stay with us again?" Zoe asked.

Josh looked up at Daniel.

"Of course he will, Zoe."

Hannah was relieved that Josh was only staying for a week. She wasn't yet ready to plan a second visit. There had certainly been a few bumps on the road during Josh's introduction to their household, although things seemed a little smoother today. It must be hard for him too, trying to fit in with a family he knew nothing about.

"Can we have dessert, Mommy?" Zoe asked.

"I think your father and I are pretty full. I'm not sure if I can finish this sandwich, but you and Josh can share a dessert if you like. Josh should get to pick it, since he's never been here before."

Josh's mouth was full, but he gave Zoe a high five.

"The cheesecake is great," Zoe whispered to him.

CHAPTER TWENTY-FOUR

B RENDA EXITED THE DELI, SLID INTO THE DRIVER'S seat of her car, and reached for her cell phone to call Henderson.

"Any progress?" she asked.

"Yeah, some. We've eliminated all but four units. Either they're occupied by Latino families, two chicks living together, or old people. Unit 204 belongs to two guys. They're married fags. Units 102 and 105 are for rent, and unit 210 is rented by an LLC. I looked for it on Air B&B and a few other short-term rental sites, but couldn't find it. Anything else you need before we go off duty?"

"Nothing else," Brenda said, disconnecting. She couldn't bring herself to say thanks, because she was too angry. She'd hoped LAPD would screen for bigots before accepting people into the Academy. It's not as if they lacked for applications. There had been a push for diversity over the past few years. There were more African Americans, Latinos, Asians and women than in the past, but clearly, this hadn't changed the attitude in the force.

She grabbed a black-and-white cookie, took a big bite,

and started her car, heading to the apartment building on Wilcox.

The address on Eddie's phone brought her to one of the newer buildings on the street. It had lower-level parking, balconies and a functioning security gate, requiring a card for entry. A list of tenants, with bells, was at the entrance, and Brenda rang the one that said Manager. A voice asked her business, and she noticed a camera mounted at the side of the gate. She gave her name, showed her police badge, and was buzzed in.

The manager's apartment was 101, and she was greeted at an open door by a middle-aged, Latina woman, in a cotton print dress.

"Angela Herrara," she said. "How can I help you?"

"May I come in?"

Angela nodded and ushered Brenda to her kitchen table. "Coffee?"

A half-empty mug was sitting on the kitchen table, along with an ash tray and a pack of cigarettes. The smell of smoke permeated the apartment.

"No thank you. I'm investigating a murder case, and I have reason to believe that one of the apartments in this building may have been the crime scene. I understand you have two vacant units, and one that is rented by a corporation. What can you tell me about them? How long have the two units been vacant, and who were the previous tenants?"

"Are you suggesting one of my tenants is a killer? That's ridiculous. This is a nice family-friendly building. What's your proof?"

"I can't discuss an open investigation. But if you don't

want to talk to me, I can come back with a warrant instead and interview all your tenants. If you cooperate and answer my questions, I won't need to bother most of them."

Angela reached for a cigarette, She didn't look pleased. "Okay, but don't bug my tenants. I'll never hear the end of it if they find out the police are looking for a murderer in our building."

"I understand. Tell me about the vacant units and I'll be as discreet as I can."

Angela reached for her lighter.

"Would you mind not smoking?"

"Why?"

"I have asthma," Brenda lied. She hated the scent of cigarette smoke.

Angela glared at her but put the lighter down. "Unit 105 has been vacant for a month. The last tenant was a young woman. She moved in with her boyfriend. The people in 102 were my next door neighbors for several years, the De Leons. They had a baby, and bought a house in Santa Clarita. That unit has only been vacant for two weeks."

"What about 204?" Brenda asked.

"Let me look that one up. I don't remember who's in which unit." Angela walked into the other room and returned with a small laptop. "Oh yeah. That's a gay couple."

"Can you describe them?"

"They're both Asian. One's about fifty. The other looks like he's in his twenties."

"And apartment 210?"

Angela frowned. "That's the corporation apartment. Nobody lives there. I've never seen a car in their spot except at night, and it's usually a different car each time. I think they use it for out of town business travelers or occasional parties. Sometimes I get noise complaints from the tenant in 209."

"That sounds promising," Brenda said.

"If you want to take a look, I've got the passkey," Angela offered.

"I'll take you up on that offer as soon as I get a warrant. Can you think of any other apartment in this building inhabited by one or two white guys with blond hair?"

Angela shook her head. "Not really."

"Do you have security cameras in the garage?"

"We have one near the elevator."

"Can you show me the video from last Sunday night?"

"No problem." Angela tapped a few keys on her laptop and turned the screen to face Brenda.

Brenda fast forwarded until a little after one AM on Monday morning. Two men wearing hoodies walked with a Black man into the elevator. They seemed to know where the camera was because they were careful to keep their faces averted.

She replayed it slowly, catching a glimpse of the Black man's profile. She was sure it was Kevin.

Fast forwarding, she found no one exiting the elevator until early Monday morning, when numerous tenants left for work.

"Is there a stairway to the garage?" she asked.

"Yeah, do you want me to show you where it is?"

"Does it have a camera nearby?"

"No, this is the only one." Angela said. "Got what you need?"

"Not quite. I have one more thing to check out and then I'll be making a copy of the files. After that, I'd appreciate you showing me the door to the stairwell."

Brenda went back to the date of Eddie's encounter and

worked her way through the footage. Once again, she saw Eddie enter the elevator with two men who were careful to avoid the camera and didn't see him leave. At least now she was positive she was in the right building.

She took a flash drive from her purse and made a copy. "I've got enough for now. You've been very helpful Mrs. Herrara. If you could just show me the stairwell, I'll be on my way. Don't say anything to anyone about this."

"Don't worry. The last thing I need is a bunch of tenants in a panic. Are we all in danger?"

"I don't think so. These murders targeted male prostitutes. Just keep your windows closed and your doors locked, as you would normally. I doubt these guys would target any of your tenants."

Angela didn't look completely convinced, but she opened the door to her apartment and pointed Brenda in the direction opposite the elevator. "The door to the stairwell is at the end of the hall. It's unlocked and the light switch is on the right."

Brenda opened the stairwell door and switched on the light. The lower part of the stairs was in shadow, and she took out her flashlight to illuminate the steps as she searched for trace evidence on the floor and along the walls. She also put on a pair of latex gloves to avoid leaving fingerprints on the banister.

Three-quarters of the way down, her patience was rewarded by a few brown stains toward the middle of a step, which repeated as she descended.

When she got to the bottom she took a small spray canister of Luminol from her purse along with a sample tube. She sprayed the nearest brown stain and shut off the light. Within a few minutes, it began to fluoresce, confirming its identity as blood.

Flipping the light back on, she sampled the adjacent spot. When she got back to the station, she'd ask the Coroner's lab to test the blood and see if it was Kevin's. In any case, she knew she had enough evidence to convince a judge to give her a warrant.

Like most experienced detectives, Brenda had a favorite judge or two. Her number one choice was assigned to the West LA District court. The court finished at three PM, and the judge could often be found in his office shortly thereafter, catching up on paperwork. If the traffic Gods were with her, it wouldn't take more than half an hour to get back to the station and make the call at the perfect time.

Brenda returned home with a warrant in her purse. It had been a productive day. To her surprise, Marcy wasn't home yet. Just as well. It was Brenda's week to provide dinner and Marcy's to clean up. Brenda preferred it the other way. Her partner was a much more imaginative chef, and Brenda's schedule often resulted in takeout from their local Chinese or Mexican restaurants.

She checked the refrigerator and pantry for an easy meal and decided on pasta and salad. She set a pot of water to boil, retrieved the linguine and a jar of Marinara sauce, and began putting together a Caesar salad. As she was whisking the dressing, Marcy arrived.

"Hi, babe. Long day?"

"Not really. I got distracted doing a computer search for wedding venues."

"Find anything?"

"Not really. I didn't know what I was looking for. Indoor or outdoor? How many guests? Price range? When?"

Brenda tossed the salad and opened a bottle of red wine. "I see what you mean. It's all connected. Personally, I'd like something small and soon."

Marcy took two wine glasses out of the cupboard and poured, handing one to Brenda. "I second that. I'd rather use our money for a great honeymoon than a big wedding."

"How big is your extended family?" Brenda asked.

"Just my parents, if they'll even come, and my favorite aunt and uncle. Yours?"

"Parents, two brothers, two sisters-in-law, and a ton of conservative religious relatives who wouldn't be caught dead at a gay wedding. I don't know if my parents and brothers will come either."

Marcy sipped her wine slowly. "Which friends would you like to invite? I've got a small group at work I'm close to."

"Daniel and Hannah, a handful of other colleagues from work, and about a half-dozen folks I've socialized with from the LGBT Center. You've met most of them."

"So, less than fifty."

"Way less," Brenda agreed.

"We could elope, go to Vegas, and get married in the Church of Elvis."

"Very funny. I hate Vegas," Brenda said.

"Seriously, we need to break the news to our families. At least that will clarify the guest list."

Brenda broke the strands of linguini in two, threw them into the pot of boiling water and set the timer for 12 minutes. "It's on my schedule. I promise I'll tell them as soon as I solve this case."

CHAPTER TWENTY-FIVE

Brenda and Alberto arrived at the Wilcox apartments a little after 9 a.m.

"You, again." Angela said. She didn't look happy as she opened the door.

"Us again, with a warrant for the apartment. May we have the passkey please?"

Angela held out her hand for the paperwork, signaled them to wait, and returned shortly with a key. "I need this back as soon as you're done."

"Yes, ma'am," Alberto said, as Angela closed her door.

"Don't touch anything," Brenda said. "We don't want to mess up any fingerprints. Put these on." She opened her crime scene kit and took out shoe covers and gloves for both of them. Then she brushed fingerprint powder on the doorknob.

"I don't see anything," Alberto said.

"I don't either. That's worrisome. Usually doorknobs are loaded with prints."

"Gloves?" Alberto suggested.

"Maybe, or the doorknob was wiped."

Brenda inserted the passkey and unlocked the bolt, opening the door.

Alberto sniffed audibly. "Smells like Clorox in here."

"Someone's been cleaning up."

The living room was dark, the blinds closed. Brenda used a pencil to flip the light switch, to avoid smearing a print with her gloved finger. The light revealed two cheap looking lamps on either side of a sofa. The furniture looked like motel quality. The only expensive item was a large, flat screen TV.

The kitchen was a small galley space, with oak cabinets and Formica countertops . The refrigerator was empty except for several six-packs of beer and two tubes of KY jelly.

The bedroom was the interesting space. There was a large bed with a wrought iron headboard and footboard. Two pairs of handcuffs hung from the headboard, and ropes were attached at either end of the footboard. The bed was neatly made with crisp, ironed white linens.

A pair of wrist irons were bolted to one wall, reminding Brenda of movie scenes in Medieval dungeons. The other wall contained a fiberboard dresser.

Alberto opened the drawers. "What is all this stuff?"

Brenda walked over to take a look. She wouldn't have known either if she hadn't done her research on BDSM sex toys.

Without touching she pointed to several items: "Nipple clamps, rubber gags, a strap-on penile cage, a bar for keeping the legs spread, an assortment of whips, and you probably recognize this as a giant dildo."

Alberto winced, and his face turned red.

"I guess we've discovered the crime scene," he said.

"This bar looks heavy enough to be the murder weapon. Remind me to tell forensics to test it," Brenda said.

She opened the lower drawers to find a supply of laundered linens.

"Someone obviously remade the bed," Alberto said. "These sheets look freshly ironed. Did you notice a washing machine in the apartment?"

"Not yet," Brenda said. "But let's check the closets."

The bedroom closet was empty, except for a few hangers, but one of the hall closets contained a combined washer-dryer. Brenda reexamined the sets of sheets. One of them was clean, but creased, and inexpertly folded.

"No one irons their own sheets. I think they send their laundry out, but this sheet set looks home washed. I'll bet they cleaned up after Kevin, made the bed, and washed the sheet he was lying on. Lucky for us, blood can still be detected after laundering. I don't think this cleanup job was done the night of the murder. They must have come back."

She took a flash drive from her supply bag and handed it to Alberto.

"I'm going to call the forensic team. Can you go down to Angela's apartment and download all of the files from the security camera, as far back as it goes? We need to see if these guys were frequent flyers, and if they were less cautious about the camera when they weren't planning to torture anyone."

"Yes, ma'am. I'm on it," Alberto said, clearly happy to leave.

Brenda was getting fond of Alberto. He was quite observant for a rookie, and he'd be an excellent cop with good mentoring. She took out her cell phone and made the call.

The forensic team arrived forty minutes later, and Brenda turned the scene over to them, hoping they'd be able to find some fingerprints and blood evidence after the cleanup. She went downstairs to the manager's apartment and retrieved Alberto and the flash drive.

"You done?" Angela asked.

"We are, but our forensic team is just beginning. When they leave, they'll return your keys. I told them to be discreet and avoid being seen in their gear by any of the tenants."

Alberto gave Angela a warm smile. "Thank you for being so helpful. We appreciate it."

To Brenda's surprise, Angela smiled back.

"Just arrest these guys so my building can get back to normal."

"We'll do our best," Alberto said, as they left.

"You're quite a charmer," Brenda said. "She was totally grumpy the entire time I spoke with her yesterday."

"My parents come from the same state as hers in Mexico," Alberto said. "That makes me practically family."

"You've got good people skills," Brenda said. "Don't become a cynic and lose them like some cops. It's hard to get witnesses to trust you, and being nice helps."

"Thanks."

Brenda started the car. "How about we grab some lunch before we head back to the station and go through those videos? My treat."

"That would be great. You pick the place."

CHAPTER TWENTY-SIX

BRENDA DECIDED ON JON AND VINNY'S, WHERE THE two of them split a Roman Gladiator pizza.

"My roommate's not much of a carnivore," Brenda said. "So glad you like real pizza."

"Pizza is a staple at our house," Alberto said.

"Are you married?" Brenda asked. She wanted to know a little more about her rookie.

"No. I'm living at home with my folks and my three younger sisters. They need the financial help, putting the girls through school, and my mother is an excellent cook. So far it works for all of us. My parents are great, and they don't pry into my personal life."

"Lucky you," Brenda said. "I come from a family of cops in West Covina. I get interrogated whenever I go out with them for dinner."

Alberto laughed and washed down a large bite with his Coke.

"You mentioned your parents came here from Mexico."

"A long time ago, when it was easier to come legally. I was born here. Where is your family from?" Alberto asked.

"My ancestors are a mix of English, Irish, Austrian and Swedish. I think they came over in the middle of the nineteenth century. I'm not one of those people who traces family genealogy. My grandparents moved to California and I grew up here," Brenda shared. "You think any of your sisters are interested in law enforcement?"

"I think right now all they're interested in is boys, but if any of them expresses an interest, I'm going to ask you to be a role model. I really appreciate how much you're teaching me."

"You're going to be an excellent detective," Brenda said, as she reached for her credit card and the check. "We'd better head back to the station and resume detecting. It's going to be a long day for me. I've got to go back to Hollywood tonight and return Eddie's phone. I promised to meet him at eight-thirty tonight, in front of the doughnut shop."

"Do you want me to come with you?" Alberto asked.

"No need. It's a short errand. I do want you to come with me Friday night though. We're going undercover to a BDSM dungeon which attracts men who like things rough. If our murderers are part of the party scene, that's the dungeon where they'd be found."

"But how will we recognize them?"

"I'm going as a mistress."

"In one of those low-cut black leather outfits?" Alberto asked.

"Something modest enough to conceal a weapon, and I'll be wearing a hidden video camera. I plan to record videos of any men who fit the description. Then we'll run them through facial recognition programs and see what we get. We may not get anything, but I thought it might be worth a try."

"What about me? Do I just circulate as a guy who wants to hook up?"

"Definitely not. I don't want to have to rescue you from whips and chains. You'll be staff, either security or a bartender. Wear a leather jacket and your shoulder holster."

"I'm hoping we aren't going to need guns," Alberto said, as they got into the car and headed west.

They reached the station in twenty minutes

"So what's the plan for the afternoon," Alberto asked. "Should we start on the video clips?"

Brenda nodded. "Why don't you sit down at Daniel's desk and take the flash drive. I've got some paperwork to finish for the murder book. Yell if you find something interesting."

Alberto tapped her shoulder half an hour later. "Check this out. I ran through the week after the murder. Mostly, lots of tenants going to work. It's easy to avoid the camera entering the elevator in the garage, but almost impossible if you're exiting. Our suspects showed up last night, after midnight, and they were careful to avert their faces. They went in the elevator but never came back down. They must have taken the stairs, like last time."

Brenda leaned over and watched the tape. "It's been nine days since the murder. Why did they wait so long to clean up after themselves?"

"I wish we'd gotten that warrant a day earlier. Bad luck."

Brenda chewed on her lower lip. Bad luck or inside information? Could Angela have tipped them off?

"Good pick up. Let me download the files to my computer. I'll start at the beginning. You work your way backwards from where you started and we'll meet in the middle."

~

By five o'clock they'd finished the files with no further useful images. Brenda extracted the clips with the suspects, put it on a new flash drive and gave it to Izzy, hoping he could sharpen the images and extract information they hadn't seen. Then she left the station, picked up chicken tandoori and a lamb biryani from her favorite Indian restaurant and headed home. She'd relax for a little while with Marcy before driving back to Hollywood.

~

"Mmmm. I love Tandoori," Marcy said. "How about after dinner we stream *The Best Exotic Marigold Hotel*? You've put me in the mood for India."

"Sorry, love. I have to go back to Hollywood and return a phone to a witness at eight-thirty. We could watch it tomorrow?"

"Unless someone else gets killed. When we get married, I've got to train you to prioritize my live body over all those dead ones." Marcy reached for a piece of Naan.

"Tomorrow, I promise. No matter how enticing a body crawling with maggots might be."

~

Brenda had no trouble parking across from the doughnut store at 8:30 at night. Santa Monica Boulevard and its crowd of prostitutes didn't come alive until later. The sheer emptiness of the street felt creepy, and she decided she was more comfortable in her car, waiting for Eddie to appear, rather than standing in front of the shop.

She waited, scanning the street in both directions, and checking her watch. By nine o'clock, she was annoyed. By nine-thirty, she was angry. To hell with Eddie. If he didn't want his phone back, it was his problem, not hers. She'd kept her word.

By now, a few guys were assuming their positions, waiting for a pickup. When she opened her car door, there was a scent of weed. She'd walk over, find one of the hookers who'd been there the other night, and leave a message for Eddie.

As she walked toward the men, she got their attention. They weren't used to women picking them up. Then one of them recognized her and waved. It was the skinny blonde guy with the long hair.

"Hey. Wha's up?"

"I'm looking for Eddie. I have something of his I wanted to return. He was supposed to meet me an hour ago."

"Shit." Two of the other hustlers moved in, listening to the conversation.

"You know where to find him?" she asked.

"Yeah," the blonde said. "He's at the County morgue. Someone stabbed him in an alley last night."

CHAPTER TWENTY-SEVEN

BRENDA WAS NOT ONE TO BELIEVE IN COINCIDENCES. Eddie's murder and the sanitized crime scene, on the same night, suggested that someone was cleaning up. That meant the perpetrators had been tipped off.

Angela was her first suspect, but she couldn't rule out Alberto. Both of them knew a forensic team was coming on Wednesday. She didn't want to believe that Alberto had betrayed her trust. She considered herself a good judge of character and she liked him, but her inner Detective had to include him as the source of the leak. Then there was McCall and Henderson. They didn't know about the forensic team, but they did know she was closing in on the crime scene.

Brenda's first call when she reached her desk Thursday morning was to Alicia Jenkins. "Tuesday night, a prostitute named Eddie, who was a witness in my homicide case, was stabbed to death in Hollywood. I was hoping you could tell me which detective caught the case."

"Oh yeah. Eddie Lee. He was a frequent flier in the sex crimes division. Only eighteen-years-old and a heroin addict. Detective Hye Kim is in charge of the case. What's the story?"

Brenda didn't know Kim. He must have joined Hollywood division after she left.

"I won't bore you with all the details, but a few weeks ago, Eddie was picked up and badly beaten by two guys who are my number one suspects in the murder of a trans man."

"You think Eddie's murder is connected to your case, and not a drug deal gone bad?"

"Let's say I'm suspicious. Can you connect me to Kim?"

"Hold on."

Brenda sat at her desk and drew doodles of her name and Marcy's with various combinations for a joint surname. Adams-Jordan, Jordan-Adams, or maybe they would each just keep their own.

"Kim here."

"It's Detective Brenda Jordan, West LA. We may have a case in common." Brenda briefly filled him in. "If I'm right, we're looking for the same killers. We should be sharing information and working together."

"I don't have much yet. Guy was stabbed, multiple times. He had heroin on him. Neither the autopsy nor the forensics are back."

"I've got his phone and a complete download of all the information on it. I used it to locate the crime scene. It's an apartment in Hollywood set up as a private BDSM dungeon. I got a warrant yesterday and did the forensics. I can send you the download, and all the information I have on my homicide. We can exchange forensics when we get them back, and keep one another in the loop."

"You know," Kim said, "Sometimes the simplest solutions are the right solutions. You're looking for zebras when the horse is right in front of you. This guy was a hooker and a serious druggie. I figure his drug dealer stabbed him. You're making my life more complicated."

"Eddie was murdered the same night the crime scene apartment was wiped clean of prints and trace. As far as I'm concerned, it suggests someone getting rid of loose ends, and someone in the know tipping off the killers. That's my working hypothesis."

"I need your download asap. His drug dealer's number is probably on his phone."

"I said I'd send it, and my forensics, when I get them. I want yours as well."

"Yeah, okay. But I don't think I'm going to need your help to solve this."

Easy for him to say. What an ass.

"Fine." Brenda got off the phone and shredded her doodles. Then she took a walk to the lab and checked on her forensics.

"Most of it isn't back yet," the tech said, "but I do have one thing for you, the murder weapon."

He put on a pair of gloves and fetched the metal bar. "We got traces of the victim's blood on it and the coroner says the shape fits the wounds in his skull."

"All right! What about the sheets?"

"The messy one had blood traces as well. We haven't done the others yet."

"Fingerprints? Footprints?" Brenda asked.

"The team didn't find any. Either they wore gloves or I'm hiring them to clean my house. We're still going through the trace evidence from the floor, bed and carpet, but who knows how many guys used this place for fun and games?"

The results were better than expected. Brenda hadn't counted on finding the murder weapon.

"Thanks," she said. "Keep me posted."

She didn't want to return to her desk, mostly because she didn't want to see Alberto just now. She'd go back to Wilcox and talk to Angela again. Maybe Angela had, deliberately or unwittingly, been the source of the leak.

"You, again." Angela didn't seem happy to see her. "What now?"

"Just a quick question," Brenda said. Angela showed no signs of inviting her in.

Brenda leaned toward her, hand on the doorframe, and waited a moment to see if invading her personal space would result in an open door. Angela stood her ground.

"Do you remember, last Tuesday, I told you I'd be back the next day with a warrant? Did you mention it to anyone?"

"Why would I? I told you, the last thing I want is for the tenants to get wind of this."

"Not your family or best friend? No one?"

"I'm divorced and my kids are grown. I live alone. There's no one to tell. Why are you asking?"

Brenda prided herself on her very accurate bullshit detector. Angela showed no signs of lying, no hesitations, no facial tells. It wasn't what she'd hoped for.

"Just making sure. Did you happen to see or hear anything out of the ordinary after midnight on Tuesday?"

"I'm in bed and asleep by ten, and I don't wake up until after seven."

"Okay, thanks. Let me know if you see anyone you don't know around the building." Brenda held out her card.

"Let me know when you catch the guy, so I can stop worrying," Angela said, stuffing the card into the pocket of her housedress.

"I will. Thanks again for your cooperation."

Brenda sat in her car and checked her phone for messages. There was nothing urgent. She should probably head back to the station, but she really didn't want to be there. Putting the car in gear, she made her decision and headed to the Farmer's Market to grab some lunch and get take-out for dinner. The last thing she felt like doing was cooking when she got home.

~

By the time Marcy arrived, Brenda had set the table, put out a bottle of Primitivo, along with some crostini as an appetizer, and was ready to reheat a large bowl of asparagus pasta with lemon sauce in the microwave.

"Smells great. Is it a special occasion?" Marcy hung up her jacket and tossed her purse on a chair.

"Had a bad day today, so I went to the Farmer's Market on the way home and bought us carbs for dinner. There's tiramisu for dessert."

"Be still my stomach!" Marcy poured them both a glass of wine. "What would you think about looking at a few wedding venues over the weekend? Or are you on call?"

"I'm not on call, and that sounds like a great idea. Daniel should be coming back on Monday, which will make life easier."

Marcy reached for a pesto crostini. "I'm almost afraid to ask how the case is coming."

"Why don't you tell me about your day instead? I'm sure it was better than mine."

Marcy took a sip of wine. "I got an interesting new client today. She's got more money than she knows what to do with, and wants to redecorate her mansion in Holmby Hills, starting with her husband's study."

"Uh-oh. Does *he* want to redecorate his study? I thought most men were possessive about their man caves."

"They are. He's out of town and it's a surprise." Marcy grinned. "I'm not planning to be around when he gets back. Who wants to be in the middle of that?"

Brenda got up from the sofa and took the salad out of the refrigerator. "Bring your wine and let's sit down."

"I thought you'd never ask." Marcy picked up both glasses and came to the table. "Your turn. What happened to upset you?"

"You were asleep when I came home last night, so I didn't get a chance to tell you. My only witness was murdered the same day we did a search of the crime scene. The Hollywood detective in charge of the guy's murder refuses to believe there could possibly be a connection between his case and mine. Getting him to cooperate is going to be a heavy lift. He wants the simplest solution and can't see beyond it."

"Dumbass," Marcy said. She reached over and squeezed Brenda's hand.

"The worst part of it is that I'm afraid there may have been a leak. The crime scene was cleaned thoroughly, and we have video of the same two guys entering the building the night before we searched it."

"Are you afraid the leak may have come from your rookie?"

Brenda nodded. "I don't want to believe it. My gut says he's a good guy and will make a good cop, but maybe my gut got it wrong."

"I've always trusted your gut. Alberto can't have been the only person at the West LA station who knew you were searching the crime scene. There's no such thing as a secret if even one other person knows. It spreads like a virus. Why don't you talk to him tomorrow and see who else might know?"

Brenda took a deep breath. Marcy always managed to calm her when she was agitated.

"By the way, speaking about tomorrow, I have to do a late shift. I'm going undercover, but I should be home before midnight."

"Maybe I should marry a bookkeeper, someone who works at a totally boring nine-to-five job."

"You could, but what fascinating stuff could she talk about over dinner? You have to know that I'd rather be with you every night, but this is what I do for a living, and most of the time I like it."

"Fighting for justice," Marcy said, finishing off her wine and pouring a second glass. "Defending the underdog."

"You could put it that way. This case, in particular, means a lot to me."

"I know, sweetheart. Where are you going?" Marcy asked.

"To a BDSM party, at a place where guys like the ones I'm looking for might be found."

"Can I go with you? I have lots of leather jackets."

"I'd get fired if I took a civilian to a place where men like it rough, especially one as attractive as you are."

"Sweet talk won't get you anywhere," Marcy said. "Promise me you'll be careful. Are we still on for wedding venues on Saturday?"

"You bet. It will be the highlight of my week."

CHAPTER TWENTY-EIGHT

BRENDA SLEPT IN AND TOOK A VERY HOT SHOWER. Mistress Rose had promised her a costume so she dressed in jeans, a t-shirt and an old fleece jacket. Then she put on a pair of black, knee-high boots into which she'd installed a sheath for a knife. She'd told Alberto to wear a shoulder holster under his jacket, but who knew if her costume would accommodate a gun. At least this way, she wouldn't be defenseless if anything happened.

In the bathroom, she opened Marcy's make-up drawer and examined the contents. Brenda never bothered with makeup, and hoped she could manage to put some on without looking too ridiculous. Too bad Marcy was at work and couldn't help.

She settled for some blush, mascara, and pink lipstick, all of which she stuffed into a pocket along with a comb. Drawing her blonde hair back, she put it up in a twist and pinned it.

Then she phoned Alberto. "Hey, it's me. I wanted to go over our plans for the evening. We need to be at the dungeon at seven to meet with Mistress Rose. I was thinking, since you live on the Eastside, it makes no sense for you to come to the station first. Why don't you meet me there?"

"Sounds good to me. Where were you all day yesterday?"

"In Hollywood, dealing with some bad news. When I went to return Eddie's phone Wednesday night, I found out he'd been murdered. I've been trying to get some cooperation from the moron who caught the case in Hollywood division. I'll update you when I see you."

She ended the call and headed into the station where she signed out a pair of attractive glasses with a hidden video camera. Looking in the mirror of the Ladies Room, she concluded that they made her look like a school teacher. She was sure Rose would have a costume to go with them. After all, what man wouldn't want to be disciplined by a sexy professor?

Alberto was waiting for her outside. He looked handsome in his black leather bomber jacket and faded jeans. A lock of black hair fell over his forehead, and his dark eyes sparkled in the light of the doorway. If she'd been straight, she'd have found him quite attractive.

"Have you been waiting long?" she asked.

"Just a few minutes. I figured we should go in together."

"I need to ask you something first," Marcy said. "Did you mention to anyone that we were getting a warrant for that Hollywood apartment?"

"Not that I can recall. Why?"

"It's bothering me that the scene was sanitized and Eddie was murdered on Tuesday night, just before we got a chance to search. It feels as if it's all connected. I've never believed in coincidence."

Alberto pursed his lips and drew his eyebrows together. "You think there's a leak? Angela perhaps?"

"I interviewed her again yesterday. She denies telling anyone, and I got the feeling she was telling the truth."

"It wasn't a secret at the station. The Captain knew, and anyone could have overheard us talking about it. But it's a bit farfetched to think some cop tipped off the killers."

Once again, Brenda's bullshit detector failed to go off. She didn't really suspect Alberto, and he had a point, although the coincidence was still gnawing at her. Just because she liked him didn't mean she could rule him out. "We should probably go in."

Alberto opened the door and held it for her. A burly security guard sat near the entrance and asked for their names.

"We're Brenda and Alberto. Mistress Rose told us to come early," Brenda said. It was best not to identify themselves as LAPD.

The guy nodded. "Go on upstairs. She's in the front parlor."

Mistress Rose was dressed in a lacy, long black dress that reminded Brenda of Victorian widows. She wore bright red lipstick and dark eye shadow, which made her eyes luminous against her white hair.

"Nice to see you, Detective. Who's your friend?"

"This is Alberto. He's also LAPD."

"Well, come on back and we'll get you set for tonight. Alberto, do you know how to mix a martini?"

"Yes, ma'am."

"Excellent. You can join our bartender and pass out the beers. Everyone gets a ticket for one free drink and then they pay. I stock beer, cheap champagne, and soft drinks."

"No martinis?"

"No martinis. Too expensive," Rose said. "I'm not running a charity here. The bar's in the main room. Go introduce yourself to the bartender as my temporary hire for tonight, and he'll get you started. You can come with me, Brenda."

Brenda followed Rose down the hall to a spacious room with racks of costumes. There was lace, sequins and leather.

"I didn't know you wore glasses," Rose said. "Can you see without them? They aren't very sexy."

"Sorry, my contact lenses were hurting and I had to take them out. Blind as a bat without my glasses."

Rose sighed. "Let's see what we can find you to wear that goes with glasses."

"I was thinking I could be a teacher. Twin sweater set, pearls and a ruler."

Rose laughed. "I have just the thing." She walked over to another rack and pulled out a voluminous, shapeless black dress. "You can go as a nun. I've got the headdress to match, and I certainly have a ruler. I bet you'll bring back fond memories for our Catholic clientele."

"That's perfect," Brenda said. It was. She could skip the makeup, wear the glasses, and had she but known, could have concealed her gun. She didn't even have to remove her jeans and t-shirt.

She slipped the habit over her head, straightened it out, and put on the wimple. Rose handed her a well used wooden ruler.

As they returned to the front room, Brenda could hear the buzz of conversation. At least thirty people were there, mixing as close to the bar as they could get. She spotted Albert passing out bottles.

The crowd was all types and all ages. There were older men in business suits, young guys with tattoos in leather, male hairstyles ranging from shaved, to pony tails, to Mohawks. They were white and black, Asian and Latino. Half a dozen beautiful women, heavily made up, wearing leather and studs, or very short, tight dresses, circulated among the men.

"My staff," Rose said. "The two big guys in blue leather are security. Let me introduce you."

"Guys, this is Mistress Brenda. She's new. See that she doesn't get into trouble, will you?" Rose looked at them with a motherly smile.

"Don't you worry, Mistress Brenda, I'll take good care of you." The bigger of the two security men said.

"Thank you. You can call me, Sister."

"Why don't we get you a tray with some champagne glasses," Rose suggested. "That way you can circulate but can avoid getting involved with any prospective clients."

"Brilliant," Brenda said.

"Unless you'd like to," Rose added.

Armed with a dozen glasses of cheap bubbly, Brenda made her way through the crowd, concentrating on meeting the white men with blond buzz cuts.

One of them was talking to a skinny black man wearing gold hoop earrings. The black man helped himself to a glass of champagne. The white man wore a leather harness, had tattoo sleeves covering both arms, and ice cold blue eyes in a pale face. She imagined him with a whip, overseeing a concentration camp.

"I don't drink that shit," he said. "Get me a beer, will you honey?"

Brenda looked up at him, making sure her glasses

recorded a good view of his face. "Sure thing. I'll be right back."

She returned to the bar, and taking the hint, replaced most of the champagne with an assortment of beers. After serving the guy with the tattoo sleeves, she made her way toward a man in a business suit with a shaved head, who was chatting up a guy in a white toupee. As Brenda drew nearer, and passed out her beers, she overheard a lively discussion about day trading.

She offered her drinks with a smile, catching their eyes, and memorializing them on the video camera in her glasses. As the evening progressed, the crowd got larger. Several of the mistresses led clients toward the back of the dungeon, and Brenda saw several male couples headed in the same direction. She worked her way from the back of the room to the bar, trying not to miss any possible suspects. The room was looking increasingly like a skinhead convention.

As she navigated the crowd on her way back to the bar, a bald businessman with a luxuriant mustache grabbed her arm.

"Hey, mistress. You remind me of my sixth grade teacher. She loved using that ruler. Want to join me at school in the back?"

Brenda flashed her most disarming smile. "I'd love to, but I've been assigned to passing out drinks. I'm sure one of the other mistresses would be happy to accommodate you."

She extracted her arm and placed her tray on the bar.

Alberto caught her eye. "Don't look now, but there's a tall, skinny guy with blonde hair behind you on your right side. He's talking to one of the mistresses."

"What about him?"

"I recognize him. We went to high school together. Why don't you go offer him a beer and get a good photo?"

"Is there something I should know?"

"Yeah, I'll tell you when we leave."

Brenda picked up her tray and meandered in the direction of the tall blonde man. This took more time than she anticipated, and she only had two beers left by the time she got there.

"Would either of you like a drink?" Brenda looked up at the man, and caught a dirty look from the mistress, who clearly thought Brenda was trying to steal her client.

The guy grinned. "Why, sister, I didn't know nuns drank." He grabbed both bottles and passed one to his companion.

The man took several gulps of his drink, and turned back to the mistress. Brenda saw them head in the direction of the private rooms.

By then, the gathering had quieted, couples had found one another, and Brenda had filmed all the possible suspects. She signaled to Alberto that she wanted to leave. With most of the mistresses occupied in the back rooms, she didn't want to fend off any more clients.

As she walked down the hall to the costume closet to return her robe, she could hear grunts of pain or pleasure in the rooms she passed. It was definitely time to get out of here.

Alberto was waiting when she emerged in her jeans and fleece jacket. They paused outside the building.

"Where are you parked?" he asked.

"Around the corner."

"I'll walk you to your car and tell you about that guy."

"Who is he?"

"When I was in high school, I lived in Orange County. Do you remember a few years ago there was a scandal? A group of boys had posted a picture on Facebook, giving the Nazi salute. They called themselves the Little Hitlers."

"That rings a bell. I think I read about it in the LA Times. What's the guy's name?"

"Garth Jackson."

"Who else was in the group?"

"Garth was the only one I knew. It was a big high school. He was a bully."

They reached Brenda's car and she opened the doors. "Get in. I'll drop you at your car. You don't happen to have your high school yearbook, do you?"

"At home."

"Bring it in on Monday. We'll see if we can find that Facebook photo and identify them from your yearbook. Maybe some of them are on my video."

"Will do." Alberto got out of her car. "Drive carefully," he said. "Have a nice weekend. See you, Monday."

"You too." Brenda pulled away and headed west.

On second thought, she couldn't wait until Monday. She'd head back to the station and start her research right now.

CHAPTER TWENTY-NINE

THE STATION WAS QUIET AT 2:00 A.M. ON SATURDAY night. The cops assigned to night patrol were out in their cars. The on call detectives were either at home, trying to sleep until they were paged, or out at a scene. The usual assortment of drunks and druggies were already in holding cells and only a handful of cars were in the parking lot.

The cop manning the front desk waved at Brenda as she walked in.

"What's up, Detective. You're not on call tonight."

"Just need to check on some information that can't wait until Monday. I won't be long," Brenda said.

She was the only person in the large room where the detectives had their cubicles. The silence was eerie. Brenda sat down at her desk and booted up her computer.

She pulled up the LA Times and searched for the Little Hitlers. She had no trouble finding the article, but there was no photograph. At least she now had the correct dates.

She could access Garth Jackson's Facebook page, but she suspected that the photo in question would have been deleted long ago. On the other hand, he may have posted more recent photos she could correlate with her video recordings.

Brenda decided she'd try the Orange County local papers first, and leave Facebook for Monday along with her videos. She slipped the video glasses into her top drawer and locked it. Then she tried the Orange County Register.

The photo was there, although the paper did not identify any of the boys who were giving the Nazi salute, wearing swastika armbands, and holding a banner identifying themselves as the *Little Hitlers*.

The article referred to their Facebook diatribe about Blacks, Latinos, Asians and Jews in their high school, but didn't quote it. It had probably been vile.

There had been an outcry from parents and teachers alike, demanding the students be expelled or suspended, and questioning why the school had permitted this group to exist. The principal denied all knowledge, and claimed to have no control over what students posted online or what their activities were outside the school. Brenda didn't bother following the story any further. She was only interested in identifying the boys.

She printed out the photo and placed it under her desk lamp. Garth was easy to recognize. Brenda focused on a close examination of each of the other faces to see if any of them were familiar from the dungeon. Suddenly her eyes widened.

She knew two of those faces, and their identity explained everything. Now, she understood why Kevin's body had been dumped at the homeless camp under the Sepulveda off ramp, and why Eddie had been murdered. She was horrified at the answer. Unfortunately, acting on it would have to wait until Monday, and she needed to get all her evidence together before making her move.

She shut down her computer, stuck the photo in her desk drawer, locked it, and waved goodbye to the cop at the desk as she walked out to the parking lot.

The lot was dark and quiet. While she'd been inside, a black SUV had parked a few spots over, blocking her view of her car. She walked around it, and fished in her purse for the remote, clicking it to unlock the door.

As Brenda approached the driver's side, she heard a noise. As she turned to see where it was coming from, she felt a hard, painful blow to the back of her head, and then everything went black.

CHAPTER THIRTY

MARCY OPENED HER EYES, STRETCHED AND ROLLED over, seeking Brenda's warm body on the other side of the bed. The sheet was cold, the pillow fluffy, and the bedcover undisturbed. Where the hell was she? Marcy glanced at her watch and saw it was just past five in the morning.

She got out of bed, slipped her feet into a pair of slippers, and headed to the kitchen, peeking into their shared study on the way to the stairs.

"Babe, are you down there?" she called as she descended.

No answer.

The kitchen was pristine, exactly as she'd left it after cleaning up the dinner dishes. Brenda's house keys and sunglasses were not on the hall table, and her car wasn't in its spot next to Marcy's in the garage.

A bolt of fear churned her stomach. Had something happened at that dungeon? Was Brenda hurt or had her cover been blown?

Marcy tried Brenda's cell. Her call went to voicemail.

Then she phoned the station. "May I speak to Detective Brenda Jordan?"

"Detective Jordan's not on call this weekend. Can I take a message?"

"This is her roommate Marcy. She never came home and I'm worried. I can't reach her."

"She was here earlier, but she left for home about three in the morning. Let me take a quick look in the parking lot and see if her car is there. What does she drive?"

"It's a new silver Chevy Volt."

Marcy waited on hold, pacing the kitchen floor, her anxiety increasing.

"Ma'am, it looks like her car is in the lot. It's locked, but she's not in the station."

"Where the hell is she?"

"I don't know. Why don't you calm down and give her a few hours to get in touch. If you don't hear from her, come down to the station and file a report around eight a.m."

Eight a.m., my ass. Marcy thanked him and ended the call. Turning back to her phone, she called Daniel's cell.

Daniel was deeply asleep and woke abruptly as his phone rang. It wasn't supposed to be ringing at this hour when he was on vacation.

"Daniel, it's Marcy. I think something bad has happened to Brenda. I need your help."

"What's wrong?"

Marcy brought him up to date. "We were supposed to visit possible wedding venues today. She wouldn't just take off for some work emergency without letting me know. I'm frightened and I don't think the guy I spoke to at the station is taking me seriously."

Daniel's muscles tensed. This wasn't like Brenda and his police gut was telling him that Marcy was right to be worried. "Meet me at the station in half an hour," Daniel said. "We'll figure this out."

Hannah, who had also been awakened by the phone, gave him a questioning look.

"That was Marcy. Brenda's missing and may be in serious trouble. I've got to go."

"Oh, my God. Tell me what I can do to help."

"Right now, explaining to the kids why I'm not here would be very helpful. I feel lousy not being able to spend Josh's last day with him."

"No guilt needed. I'll just tell Josh the truth and I'm sure he'll understand."

"Thanks sweetheart." Daniel bent and kissed her lips.

Hannah stood up and gave him a long hug. "Please keep me posted. You know I love Brenda too."

CHAPTER THIRTY-ONE

W HEN DANIEL PULLED IN TO THE STATION PARKING lot he spotted Marcy's bright red Mazda, and Marcy pacing in front of the back door. As he exited his car, she ran to him.

"Thank God, you're here. I hate cops who tell me not to worry."

"Let's go inside and talk to the guy at the front desk," Daniel said.

"I told him I was Brenda's roommate, not her fiancé, by the way. Didn't want to out her before she was ready."

"Not to worry. Do you know where she went last night, and with whom?"

"She's been mentoring this rookie named Alberto Figueroa. I don't know where the dungeon is, but Figueroa should, unless he's missing as well."

Daniel opened the back door and ushered Marcy inside. "We'll call him, as soon as I get the timeline from the desk sergeant."

He led her through a long corridor and past another set

of double doors to the front waiting room, empty at this predawn hour.

"Hey Detective Ross, you're here early. I thought you were on vacation until Monday."

"I am on vacation, but I hear Brenda may be missing. When did you last see her?"

"I didn't make note of the time. She dropped in around two a.m. and said there were a few things she needed to check on her computer. She left about an hour later."

"Was Figueroa with her?"

"Nope, she was alone."

"Did she seem upset or worried?"

"She seemed energized, like a bloodhound on the trail. You know how you guys get when you have a break in a case."

Daniel took out his phone. "You got Figueroa's cell number?"

The desk sergeant touched a few computer keys and wrote the number down on a post-it note, handing it to Daniel through the window.

"Let's go back to my desk," Daniel said to Marcy.

She followed him as he weaved his way through the rows of desks, finally seating himself on a well-worn black office chair.

"Have a seat. Brenda's desk is right there." He pointed to the desk on his right. As usual, her desk was pristine, the computer shut down, and no loose paperwork cluttering its surface. The same would not usually be said for Daniel's desk, but he'd cleaned up before his vacation. Putting his phone on speaker, he punched in Alberto's number.

"Yeah...who's this?" The voice sounded half asleep.

"Figueroa, it's Detective Ross, Brenda's partner. You awake?"

"I am now. Is something wrong?"

"Brenda may be missing. When did you last see her?"

Alberto sounded wide awake now. "How can she be missing? We did some undercover work together last night. I walked her to her car and she took off for home."

"She never made it home. She stopped into the station, did some work at her desk and left, but her car is still in the station parking lot and she's not answering her phone. Her roommate's worried, and so am I."

"That makes three of us. I'm leaving now. It shouldn't take me more than half an hour to get to the station. I want to help."

"Okay, see you when you get here." Daniel disconnected. "Change seats with me. I want to see what's on her computer from last night."

Daniel turned it on and it displayed the login page.

"Do you know her password?" Marcy asked.

"Yeah. We have one another's. Makes the job easier." Daniel logged in and pulled up the browser.

"What was she looking at?" Marcy asked.

"LA Times and Orange County Register." Daniel stared at the screen and pressed print. A printer in the corner of the room began to spit out pages.

"I'll get them." Marcy retrieved the papers, handed Daniel the printout, and peered over his shoulder.

"Little Hitlers, what's that about?"

"Apparently some kind of lead. Maybe Figueroa knows." He stared at the photo of the well-groomed, high school boys giving the Nazi salute. None of the faces looked familiar.

"This happened several years ago. Bunch of little white supremacists, showing off on Facebook. I'm puzzled as to how this fits in to her case."

He began a search of Brenda's drawers. The top one was locked.

"I suppose you have her keys," Marcy said.

Daniel shook his head. "I don't. She doesn't usually lock it."

He turned to his own desk and rummaged through the bottom drawer, removing several energy bars and a bag of M&M's. At the very back was a set of lock picks.

"They teach you this in detective school?"

"Learned it from a Lieutenant, who was taught by some burglar he arrested." Daniel fiddled with the picks and the lock clicked. The drawer contained some neatly arranged office supplies, a printout of the Little Hitlers photo, and a pair of glasses.

"When did Brenda start needing glasses?" he asked.

"She doesn't." Marcy reached for the glasses and tried them on. "They aren't prescription."

Daniel retrieved them. "They must be video glasses. We use them for undercover recording, along with other clever devices. She must have worn them last night. We need to get the video downloaded."

He looked at his watch. "Izzy, our computer guy, has the special cables for these. He should be in soon. Why don't we head to the kitchen. We could both use some coffee."

The night shift coffee pot was almost empty. Daniel rinsed it out and put fresh grounds from the giant Folgers can into the coffee maker. When it was done, he poured out two large mugs for himself and Marcy.

"I probably shouldn't be drinking this. I'm already wired," she said, as she took a large gulp.

Daniel handed her an energy bar. "Eat this. It'll dilute the caffeine."

He opened another bar for himself, and chewed slowly as he drank his own coffee.

"Let's see if Figueroa is in yet."

A dark haired man was sitting at Daniel's desk, looking at the printout of the Little Hitler's photo.

"Are you Figueroa?" Daniel asked.

Alberto nodded.

"That picture mean anything to you?"

"Yeah. I should have known Brenda couldn't wait until Monday to look this up. When we were at the dungeon, I recognized one of the guys there. His name is Garth Jackson, and I went to High School with him. He was one of a group of racist bully boys."

Alberto pointed to one of the figures. "That's Garth. I don't know the names of the rest of them, but I brought my high school yearbook with me. I'd promised Brenda to bring it Monday."

"Good thinking," Daniel said.

The morning shift of detectives and civilian office personnel had begun to arrive. There were snatches of conversation, and Daniel noticed a light in Izzy's office.

"Why don't you start seeing if you can identify the rest of the guys in that picture? I need to talk to our IT guy. This is Marcy, by the way. She's Brenda's roommate. She's going to help you look."

Daniel took the glasses and headed to Izzy's office. Izzy promised to get right on it. Then, Daniel went across the hall to brief the chief.

When he returned to his desk, he found Alberto looking numb, with his head in his hands. Marcy was seated close by, focused on Daniel's computer screen.

"What?" Daniel said.

Alberto looked up. "I Googled Garth, and identified all the guys from the yearbook. I think I might know why Brenda is missing, and who took her."

CHAPTER THIRTY-TWO

B RENDA WOKE WITH A SPLITTING HEADACHE AND AN overwhelming urge to pee . She reached back to touch her head, and her hand came away slippery with blood. The blow must have cut her scalp, and possibly fractured her skull.

Slowly, she opened her eyes only to find that it was pitch dark. Had the blow caused her to bleed into her brain and destroy her vision, or was she just in an unlit space?

She explored her surroundings with her hands and found herself lying on a narrow mattress on a rough concrete floor. The smell of urine was repulsive. Others must have been held here.

Taking a deep breath through her mouth, she attempted to sit. A wave of dizziness attacked her. She drew up her knees and bent forward, resting her head and waiting for the sensation to subside. The space was no lighter, even though her eyes, if they were working, had had time to adjust to the dark.

Brenda ran her hands over her body. She was still dressed in her jacket, jeans and boots. Her cell phone was in her back pocket. Apparently she hadn't been searched. She felt for the button, and turned it on. To her immense relief, the screen lit up. There was still plenty of battery to power the flashlight app.

She found herself in a small, underground room. There were no windows, just a door at the other end, above a flight of stairs. There was a bucket in the corner, where the smell of sewage was strongest. Holding her breath, Brenda pulled down her jeans, squatted and urinated.

As Brenda stood up and breathed, a wave of nausea and dizziness forced her to her knees and she retched into the bucket. Her stomach was empty and her retching produced mostly dry heaves. When it was over she began breathing through her mouth, unable to tolerate the combined smell of sewage and vomit. This time she got up more slowly. She couldn't risk hitting her head again in a fall.

There was a single light bulb on the ceiling, with an attached string. She walked over and pulled it. A quick glance around the room revealed that it was completely empty, except for the blood-stained mattress. Some of the blood was clearly hers, because it was red and wet, but there was evidence of old, dark, dried stains that spoke of other captives.

Turning to her phone, she checked for cell service and Wi-Fi. There was none. She couldn't call for help or text. Maybe whoever took her didn't bother taking her cell because they knew she wouldn't be able to use it.

She hadn't taken a gun to the dungeon, but the knife she had slipped into her knee- high boots was still there. Whoever had taken her had missed it. He, or they, would come here eventually, and she wasn't going to go down without a fight.

Brenda still had a splitting headache, but she was less

dizzy. Her muscles felt weak. If she was going to fight, she needed to rest. The thought of returning to that mattress was revolting. Finding a spot on the floor, out of the line of sight of the door, she turned off the room light, made her way cautiously to the wall, and sat down. Turning off her phone, she replaced it in her pocket. When she escaped, she'd need the battery.

The concrete was cold and grainy, even through her jeans. Brenda leaned back to rest her head against the wall, and felt something move along her cheek. She jerked forward, brushing at her face, and reaching for the phone. The flashlight revealed a spider web, but no spider.

Relieved, Brenda moved over a few inches and leaned back again, replacing the phone in her jeans. Then she reached for her knife and held it.

Eventually, someone would come, and she would be ready.

CHAPTER THIRTY-THREE

"Don't just sit there like a monument. Spill," Daniel said.

He wasn't sure he trusted Alberto. He'd been the last person to see Brenda. Who's to say he hadn't followed and kidnapped her?

Alberto held the printout of the photo up against the computer screen. "All of these guys went into law enforcement. Garth is in the Orange County Sheriff's office. This guy is in San Diego PD, and the one standing next to him works in San Bernardino. The two at the end are LAPD. I didn't recognize them in the photo. They both bulked up and have buzz cuts now, but they're here, at West LA Station."

"Are you suggesting they grabbed Brenda?" Daniel asked.

"I'm trying to put it together. The guys who killed Kevin drove the body all the way to West LA, where they dumped him in a homeless encampment under the 405. Why did they do that? There are plenty of places in Hollywood to dump a body."

Daniel chewed on his lower lip, trying to make sense of it.

"I'm not sure I follow your reasoning. You recognize an old racist classmate from high school in the hard-core dungeon, and just because he hung out with two other racists in high school, who happen to have joined the LAPD, you assume they're your killers? Where's your evidence?"

"I don't have any hard evidence," Alberto said, "but, if my hunch is right, dumping the body here makes sense. In Hollywood, the police have a lot more contacts for tracing down a trans John Doe. Maybe they assumed we wouldn't bother and the case would go cold."

Alberto's argument was clever. Maybe it was because he was the one who had dumped the body. He appeared concerned about Brenda, but perhaps he was just a good actor, trying to frame his fellow rookies. Daniel wasn't ready to let him off the hook.

"Whoever did this underestimated Brenda," Daniel said. "She's very persistent, and she was at Hollywood PD before she transferred here."

"She told me," Alberto said. "She had lots of Hollywood contacts, and she's so smart. We've gotta find her."

Daniel nodded.

Alberto continued. "Maybe they thought that by dumping the body and making it a Westside case, they could keep track of it, and derail things if we got too close. That could explain why Eddie was murdered. Both Henderson and McCall helped out when we needed extra hands, so they knew we'd found the private dungeon. Did you ever work with them?"

Daniel shook his head. "They're brand new. I don't know them."

"I didn't know them in high school either. It was a big

school. I was Latino. We hung out with one another, not with the white Orange County boys."

"It's a reach," Daniel said. "But how about we look at the work schedule for the nights Kevin and Eddie were murdered, and see if those guys were off? We can also track their phones and see where they were."

"You should also see if they were off last night and today," Alberto added.

"So what now? How are you going to find her?" Marcy asked.

"I have a plan," Daniel said. "The first thing I want to do is assign a cop I trust to go home with you and protect you if necessary. I also think you should be there if Brenda shows up."

"You're not going to let me help? You wouldn't even know she was missing if I hadn't called you."

"You already have helped, Marcy. I can't take a civilian with me when I go looking, and you don't have clearance for any of the databases I need to look at. There's nothing further you can do."

"Is that what you told Hannah every time she helped you solve a case?"

"Marcy, I don't want to get distracted, worrying that you might be a target, because the people who took Brenda think she told you something. I promise I'll let you know as soon as I learn anything."

Marcy frowned. "Okay, I know when I've been outmaneuvered."

With Marcy safely in the hands of a policewoman, Daniel turned to his computer.

"I'll check the work schedule. You get onto the DMV and see what kind of car each of them drives and where they live."

Alberto nodded, and the two of them turned to the computers. Daniel refilled his coffee.

After about twenty minutes, Alberto said "Henderson lives in a house in Silver Lake, and drives a white jeep Cherokee. McCall has a Hollywood apartment and drives a black Ford Explorer."

"Both of them were off yesterday, and the nights Kevin and Eddie were murdered," Daniel said.

He'd also checked on Alberto's schedule. Alberto had been off duty the night of Kevin's murder, but patrolling with another officer the night Eddie had been killed. That didn't mean he could be trusted.

"That still doesn't prove anything," Alberto said. "We're going to look pretty stupid if we're wrong."

"I'd rather be stupid than have something bad happen to Brenda."

Daniel debated his next step. He needed to get their phone records and trace their movements last night, but that could take more time than Brenda might have. If one or both of them grabbed her, what was the most likely place they would take her? Probably not to the private dungeon, because its location was known. The house in Silver Lake was a possibility, but they could never get a search warrant for it.

"Let's go see if Izzy found anything useful on the video," Daniel said. "Then I'm going to have a chat with the Chief."

"And say what?"

"That Brenda is missing and we need all hands on board to help with the search. I'll phone McCall and Henderson myself. That'll empty their homes, and we can check to see if she's locked up in there."

"Without a warrant? You think the Chief would go for that?"Alberto asked.

"The Chief doesn't have to know We could get in trouble if we're wrong. You don't have to come," Daniel said.

"It's Brenda we're talking about. I'm in."

CHAPTER THIRTY-FOUR

T HE SOUND OF FOOTSTEPS AND THE OPENING OF A door jarred Brenda out of a drowsy, half-slumber. She stood up silently, holding her knife at her side. The room light flashed on, from what must have been a switch at the top of the stairs. She squinted, trying to adjust to the sudden brightness. Someone was descending.

"Where are you, bitch?" a familiar voice asked.

A tall, muscled man, wearing a ski mask, descended the stairs. As he came into view, Brenda turned to meet him, her knife hand concealed between her thigh and the wall.

"You can take off the mask, Henderson. I recognize your voice."

Henderson pulled it off and faced her. His holster and gun were at his waist. "There you are."

"Assaulting and kidnapping a police officer is a bad idea," Brenda said, keeping her voice even and calm. "You've got to know the whole West LA station is probably looking for me as we speak. What's this about?"

"You know exactly what it's about. You couldn't just let it

go, could you? John Doe. Accidental death. End of story. No, you had to keep digging. The vic's a trannie. Who cares?"

"I care about all my victims," Brenda said. "It's my job."

"It's my job to keep trash from contaminating our streets. You should be on my side. You're a hot white girl with everything going for you. Why'd you waste your time trying to solve this case?"

"Why were you wasting your time, trying to stop me?"

"We decided you should be stopped," Henderson said.

"Who's we?" Brenda asked. "You and McCall?"

"Let's just say, we think cops should focus on keeping the world safe for good, white, Christian men and women."

"I thought Christians were supposed to love one another," Brenda said.

"We do. We just don't love the inferiors. The country would be much safer and better if we could get rid of them all." He moved closer.

"I see. Was it you two Little Hitlers who killed Kevin Chase? Did you torture him in your dungeon and dump the body under the freeway?"

Henderson smiled. "Aren't you clever? Too bad you can't tell anyone."

Brenda took a step back and tightened her hold on the knife. "You planning to kill me?"

"You haven't given me much choice. This time, I'll dump your body where it won't be found for decades." Henderson drew his gun and pointed it at her.

Brenda stepped away from the wall to give herself room to move.

"You planning to fight me? I outweigh you by fifty pounds. I'm not going to kill you yet. I'm going to fuck you first, and then kill you." He moved toward her, arms out, ready to grab her.

Brenda ran toward him, elbowed him in the chest, and plunged her knife into the center of his belly. When she pulled it out, a gush of blood splashed onto her leather jacket.

He screamed, clutching his wound and rolling on the floor.

Brenda didn't waste time. She ran around him, and stumbled up the stairs, fighting a wave of dizziness. As she reached the door, two shots rang out, the bullets hitting the wall inches from her head.

She found herself in a filthy kitchen, piled with old take-out boxes and dirty dishes. A roach scuttled across the floor from under the cabinet. The smell was rancid grease.

There was a back door, and it was unlocked. She was in a side alley between two homes on a steep hill. Holding onto the wall for balance, Brenda made her way to the street and began walking down. She didn't know where she was, and the name on the street sign was unfamiliar, but as long as she kept descending, she figured she'd hit a main street with traffic.

Her head throbbed, and her pace was unsteady. She was too dizzy to run, and she was afraid to stop long enough to search for a cell signal and call for help. She had no idea if Henderson was alone in the house, or if one of his buddies would hear him scream and come after her. She paused for a second to replace her knife in her boot. If someone saw her, they would think she was a crazy lady, carrying a knife covered in blood.

The street was quiet. Of course. It was early Saturday morning. Everyone was sleeping in. No one would let a bloody stranger into their home, if she rang a doorbell and asked for help. Her lungs burned, and she felt as if she were going to pass out.

The road curved to the right, and as she rounded the corner, she saw a car speeding up the hill. Should she duck behind the nearest hedge, or try to pretend she was out for an exercise walk? What if Henderson's co-conspirators were headed to his home?

Brenda looked frantically for a place to hide. Her head ached, her legs wobbled, her vision blurred. She slid against a tall fence and lost consciousness, face down on the concrete.

CHAPTER THIRTY-FIVE

"For God sake, slow down," Alberto shouted. "You can't do sixty on these switchbacks. You'll kill both of us."

Daniel took his foot off the accelerator and slowed to a sedate thirty miles an hour. Alberto was right, but his adrenaline was in high gear, and he could barely wait until they reached Henderson's house.

"That's better. At least now I can read the addresses."

"Try calling Henderson again," Daniel said.

"Okay, but he's not picking up. I've left six voicemail messages, telling him to come to the station asap." Alberto hit the number again. "What are you planning to say if he's home when you ring the doorbell?"

"I'll give him hell for not answering his phone and tell him to get in his car and report in immediately," Daniel said. He was also planning to break in and search the house as soon as Henderson left.

"And if no one answers?" Alberto asked.

"Then we do a welfare check and search for Brenda."

Alberto looked at the GPS screen. "We're almost there. Maybe two blocks. What's that?"

"What?"

"Can you pull over? Looks like someone lying on the side of the road."

Daniel pulled over and stopped the car. The two men got out, and Daniel saw what had caught Alberto's attention.

A woman was lying face down. He saw a pair of black, knee-high boots, jeans and a black leather jacket. Her blonde hair was matted with blood. He ran over, knelt down, and grabbed a wrist. There was a pulse.

"Is it Brenda?" Alberto asked.

Daniel turned the figure gently onto her back. Brenda looked limp and pale. Her face was bruised. He touched her bleeding head, trying to feel for a skull fracture. How badly was she hurt?

"Brenda, wake up. It's Daniel."

Brenda's eyelids fluttered. "Daniel?"

"Let's get you to the hospital."

The two men helped her to sit up, and Daniel lifted her into his arms. Alberto opened the back door of the car, and they laid her on the seat.

"Daniel. Henderson." Brenda whispered

"What about him?"

Tears trickled down Brenda's face. "I think I might have killed him. He's in the basement. Send some cops and an ambulance. He's armed, and I stabbed him."

"I'll call for medical and backup," Alberto said. "Was it Henderson who kidnapped you?"

Brenda nodded. "He admitted to killing Kevin Chase. I was next on his cover up list. What if he's dead? I've never killed anyone before."

"Don't worry about him now," Daniel said. "If he's dead,

you stabbed him in self defense. I'm taking you to Memorial."

"Call Marcy. She's going to wake up and find me gone, and she'll be so worried."

"She already is worried," Daniel said as he helped Brenda into the car. "She called me at five a.m. to tell me you were missing."

"Pass me your phone," Alberto said.

Daniel handed his phone to Alberto, who dialed Brenda's home number, and turned on the speaker, as Daniel got behind the wheel and turned the car around.

"Marcy. It's me. I'm okay. I've just got a gash that needs some stitches so Daniel's taking me to Memorial. I'll be home soon."

"Oh, my God. I was so worried. I'll meet you in the emergency room."

"You don't have to come, babe. Daniel can drive me back."

"Of course, I have to come. You can tell me everything when I get there. Can I talk to Daniel?"

"I'm driving, Marcy," Daniel said. "Brenda will be okay. I promise. I'll see you at the hospital."

"Speaking of the hospital," Daniel said, "Alberto, call Hannah on my home number. I think she should meet us there. If there's any red tape in the ER, she can cut through it."

"Great idea," Brenda said. "Maybe she can sew up my scalp."

The emergency room at Memorial was relatively quiet on this early Saturday morning. Daniel and an orderly lifted Brenda out of the car and transferred her to a gurney.

"She's a cop," Daniel said, showing the orderly his badge. "She was abducted and assaulted earlier today. There's a large gash on the back of her head."

"Let's get her admitted to the ER, and over to the CT scanner," a young doctor said. "We'll do a total body CT to check for fractures, internal injuries and any bleeding into her brain."

He approached Brenda and began taking her history. Her voice sounded coherent and stronger to Daniel, and he breathed a sigh of relief.

Stepping over to a quiet corner he phoned Hannah.

"I'm on my way," she said. "I dropped Josh and Zoe at Andrea's house. How badly is Brenda hurt?"

"They're doing the CT scans now. I'm planning to wait with Brenda until you and Marcy get here, and then I'm headed to the station. There are a couple of crooked cops I need to arrest."

CHAPTER THIRTY-SIX

B RENDA LAY, EYES CLOSED, HEAD THROBBING, AND listened to the sound of the CT scanner imaging her head and body. How had she ever managed to stand up, defend herself, and escape Henderson? If she stood up now, she was sure she would pass out. She was under no illusions as to the possible damage from the blow on her head. She could have a fractured skull, brain damage, or a bleed. What if they told her she needed brain surgery?

The sound of the machine stopped and she felt herself being transferred to a gurney. She kept her eyes closed as they wheeled her down the hall and back to the exam room. When she opened her eyes, she found Hannah sitting beside her. Hannah was wearing scrubs, her white coat, and a hospital ID badge.

"Thank God you're here. If I need brain surgery, would you pick the surgeon? I don't want just anyone poking around in my head."

Hannah got up, smiling, and took Brenda's hand. "Let's not get ahead of ourselves. The radiologist has to read your scan before we do anything."

"Where's Daniel?"

"He waited until I got here, and went back to the station. Something about arresting crooked cops."

"Is Marcy here?"

"She's on her way." Hannah took a tiny flashlight out of her pocket and bent down, examining each of Brenda's pupils. "Well, your pupils are equal in size and respond to light."

"What does that mean?"

"It means you don't have a massive hemorrhage. Can you tell me your name and where you are?"

Brenda complied.

"What year is it?"

"2015."

"Do you know who the President is?"

"Obama."

"Okay. That's all the neurological exam I remember. I have asked a real neurologist to come evaluate you."

"Can you sew up my head without shaving all my hair?" Brenda asked.

"Why don't I see if I can find the radiologist, and I'll ask the ER doc in charge of your case if he'd like me to sew you up. It looks pretty busy out there, and he might like the help, but I shouldn't step on his toes. I'll be back in a few minutes."

Brenda closed her eyes again and took a deep breath. She felt better already. It was so reassuring to have Hannah there. She'd been feeling powerless and out of control. Now she was calmer.

"Sweetheart, are you okay?" Marcy's arms were around her and hugging her hard.

Brenda's eyes filled with tears. "You came."

"Of course, I did."

"My head is covered in blood. Don't get it on you," Brenda said.

"I don't care. Tell me what happened. I've been a wreck since you failed to come home."

"I was at the station parking lot, getting into my car, and got hit on my head. I woke up in a filthy basement somewhere. Fortunately I'd stashed a knife in my boot and hadn't been searched. When the guy who nabbed me came downstairs with rape on his mind, I stabbed him and left. I just hope I didn't kill him."

Marcy grinned. "You are such a badass. I hope you did kill him. He deserved it."

"If he's dead, we can't question him, and I think he's part of something much bigger. I wasn't trying to kill him, honestly. I don't ever want to be one of those cops who think it's okay to take someone's life, even if that someone is a dirtball."

"I never thought you were." Marcy brushed Brenda's hair back from her face and bestowed a kiss on her cheek. Brenda reached up and pulled Marcy's mouth to hers.

"Get a room, guys," Hannah said as she entered.

"We've got a room," Brenda answered.

"Good news. No skull or other fractures, no internal bleeding, nothing requiring surgery. You have a tiny epidural hematoma. That's a small brain bleed. It should resolve on its own, but the neurologist will probably want to keep you overnight and repeat the CT scan of your head in the morning."

"That's a relief. Can you sew up my head? I'd rather have you do it than some intern."

"Absolutely."

"What can I do?" Marcy asked.

"While she's sewing, could you run to the cafeteria and get me a vanilla latte and a doughnut? I'm starving."

As Daniel and Alberto left the hospital, Alberto's phone rang.

"Great. Thanks for letting me know. I'm going to give the phone to Detective Ross. He's in charge of the case," Alberto said. "It's the guy from Hollywood station who went to Henderson's house."

Daniel took the phone. "Thanks for helping out. What's the status?"

"We found your guy unconscious and bleeding, but alive. The ambulance took him to Hollywood Presbyterian. He's in surgery now. I don't know if he's going to make it or not."

"Could you leave one of your guys there to guard him? I'll send someone from West LA Station to take over. Thanks."

Daniel hung up. "The Chief isn't going to be happy when he finds out what happened."

"Shouldn't we call and tell him to call off the search for Brenda?" Alberto asked.

"I'd rather tell him in person, and I don't want McCall to find out we found her before we get the chance to question him."

Chief Gabriel Tucker was an African American LAPD veteran in his sixties. He was a large man, whose toned body had developed a paunch as he moved into the administrative ranks. His head was bald and shiny, and his mustache voluminous and gray. As he listened to Daniel, he leaned forward, elbows on his desk, eyes completely focused.

"You're telling me that we have a killer in my police department, possibly two? And that Brenda was assaulted and abducted in my lot? That she escaped and stabbed Henderson, who may, or may not, survive?"

"Yes, sir. It's possible that it goes deeper than that. Henderson and McCall were part of a white supremacist group in high school. Everyone in that group now works in law enforcement."

"Just what I need. A bunch of God damned racists in my department. How's Brenda doing? Is she going to be okay?"

"I hope so, sir. She was getting a CT scan when I left, and I asked my wife, who is a doctor on staff at Memorial, to come and be with her. I'm sure she'll call me if the results show anything potentially deadly."

"You know I'm going to have to put her on leave while we investigate the stabbing," Chief Tucker said. "She'll have to see a department therapist."

"I think that's a good idea. Any officer who kills or wounds someone, especially a fellow cop, has got to be traumatized by the experience. Detective Jordan is not the kind of person who would take that likely."

Tucker nodded. "What's your next move, Ross?"

"I asked Izzy to look at the recording Brenda made under cover and see if he could identify anyone. I'd like to know if he found anything of value, and then I should interview McCall. We know our victim was taken by two people and that Henderson was one. McCall is his partner and both of them were off duty the day of the hate crime, and the day that our witness was found dead."

Tucker pressed his intercom. "Send Izzy Washington in here please."

~

"Hey Izzy," Daniel said. "The chief and I need to know if you found anything interesting on Brenda's video."

Izzy took a seat. "Facial recognition was very helpful. Brenda's video was like a Ku Klux Klan convention. Almost everyone she filmed was a radical right winger. Four of them were in law enforcement, in police or sheriff's departments in Southern California. I took a deep dive into their social media. All four are connected with white supremacist groups like the Oath Keepers or Proud Boys. Their stop and arrest records are heavily weighted toward black and brown suspects."

"Why am I not surprised?" the Chief said. "The question is does law enforcement just attract guys with those views, or are these organizations deliberately placing their members in police departments?"

"If there's any evidence of a conspiracy to control law enforcement by these groups, we'd better get to the bottom of it," Daniel said.

"Agreed," Izzy said. "I traced the social media for two of our rookies who were in the newspaper photo, Henderson and McCall. They're both involved in Aryan Nations."

"Shit," Chief Tucker said. "What morons accepted these guys into the Academy? Aren't we supposed to screen for this sort of thing?"

"I don't know," Izzy said. "Do we?"

The Chief turned to Daniel. "You and I better have a chat with McCall."

CHAPTER THIRTY-SEVEN

"McCall, the Chief would like a word," Daniel said, motioning him down the hall and preceding him.

"What's up?" McCall asked, as if a rookie being called to see Chief Tucker was an everyday occurrence.

"He wants to ask you a few questions."

"Isn't his office that way?"

"We're going to talk in here." Daniel held a door open and followed McCall into the room. It was an interrogation room, and the chief was waiting.

"Have a seat," Tucker said, motioning McCall to a single chair on the opposite side of the table. Daniel seated himself next to the chief.

"Before we get started, I want to do this by the book. I'm going to record this conversation, and Detective Ross here is going to read you your rights," Chief Tucker said.

"What's this about? I haven't done anything," McCall said.

"That remains to be seen," the Chief replied.

Daniel read McCall his rights and Chief Tucker began the questioning.

"You and Henderson were scheduled to be in today, but we haven't been able to reach him. Ross here has called his cell a dozen times. Any idea where he could be?"

McCall shook his head. "I'm sorry, sir. I've been wondering the same thing myself."

"When was the last time you saw him?"

"Friday night, when we got off shift. We grabbed a pizza together and I headed home."

"You and Henderson good friends?" Daniel asked.

McCall shrugged. "We're partners. Don't know much about his personal life."

The tone of voice was light and casual, but the body language told a different story. McCall's arms were crossed, his legs tight together. He was clearly tense and defensive.

Time to play bad cop. Daniel leaned forward. "The two of you were at the Academy together, and went to the same high school. I would have thought that made a bond."

"It was a big high school."

"So, you didn't belong to any of the same teams or clubs?"

"Not that I recall."

"How about the *Little Hitlers*?" Daniel asked. He reached into his pocket for the newspaper photo and handed it to McCall. "Sure looks like you were buddies there."

"That was a long time ago," McCall said. "Am I being accused of something? I haven't done anything wrong."

"That's not what your partner said."

"What are you talking about?"

"So, McCall," the Chief said. "What's this I hear about you two being card-carrying members of the Aryan Nation?"

"We have free speech in this country. You can't punish me or fire me because of my politics. My views are my business. We're a country of free speech."

"Speech is one thing," Tucker said. "Abducting, torturing and killing people you don't like is something else entirely. We found your partner. He confessed to killing Kevin Chase and said it was your idea."

"He also said you were the one who suggested abducting Detective Jordan because she was getting too close to solving the crime," Daniel said.

"Henderson's a liar."

"Really? He seemed determined to pin all this on you. You might want to consider cooperating with us. If Henderson was lying, you'll be much better off if you tell us the truth. Whose car did you use to take her to his house?"

"I'm not saying one more thing without a lawyer."

"Fine," Tucker said.

Chief Tucker and Daniel left the room and instructed two cops to escort McCall to a cell.

"I'd better call back all those cops who are searching for Brenda and let them know you found her," Chief Tucker said.

"I'll impound both their cars and have them gone over by a forensic team. I'm sure we'll find traces of Brenda's DNA, and if we're really lucky, we might get Kevin Chase's and some of their other victims."

Tucker nodded. "Get a search warrant for Henderson's house and have forensics go over it as well. And Ross, call both hospitals and find out what's going on with Henderson and with Brenda."

"I will, sir, and then, if you don't mind, I'm going to head home. I'm supposed to be on vacation until Monday, and my son flies back to his mother tomorrow. I'd like to spend the rest of the day with him."

"You do that, Ross." The Chief laid a hand on his shoulder. "Good work."

CHAPTER THIRTY-EIGHT

H ANNAH PULLED HER CAR UP TO THE FRONT OF HER best friend Andrea's Spanish Revival home and rang the bell. Andrea, wearing gray sweats, her blonde hair in a pony tail, greeted Hannah at the door. "I wasn't expecting you back so early. Is everything okay?"

"For now. Brenda's being admitted for overnight observation because she does have a tiny brain bleed, but I think it's stable, and she'll probably go home tomorrow. Marcy is with her. Where are the kids?"

"Josh is out back, playing basketball. Zoe is in Molly's room. They're playing with the cat."

"I appreciate this. I felt guilty leaving Josh on his last full day here, but I didn't have a choice."

Andrea led Hannah into the kitchen. "Do you have time for a cup of tea?"

Hannah collapsed into a chair. "Yes, please."

Andrea handed her a mug of Darjeeling and a small plate of shortbread cookies. Hannah reached for one and her eyes filled with tears.

"I don't think cookies are going to fix this week."

Andrea reached out and took her hand. "Tell me what's going on."

Hannah put down her tea and wiped her eyes with her sleeve. "I've been so scared for Brenda. It reminded me of when that psychotic patient of yours kidnapped you."

"I still have nightmares. I'm sure Brenda will as well. It's not easy to get past a trauma like that."

"Brenda's not all. Don't tell Daniel I said this, but I can't wait for Josh to leave. Teenaged boys are like a black hole to me. I don't know what to say, or how to act, and I feel like I'm walking on eggshells around him."

"He seems like a nice kid," Andrea says. "Is he?"

"Who the hell knows? He stole his mother's marijuana and smoked it in our house. When we took him to the beach, he spent his time ogling the girls in bikinis and making comments about their bodies. I wanted to tell him to shut up, but I thought that was Daniel's job, and he didn't say a thing."

"Daniel's probably walking on eggshells too, Hannah. This can't be easy for him, and it can't be easy for Josh."

"We tried so hard to take him all over the city to places we thought he'd enjoy, but he just seemed bored."

"Remember back to when you were a teenager. I'm sure all you wanted to do was to hang out with your friends, not spend a week with adults you barely know. Josh has no friends here, because he doesn't live here. I bet he's looking forward to going home tomorrow."

"At least we both agree on that. The truth is, right now, I don't want another person in our family. I wanted Daniel's and my baby. It's been six months since my miscarriage. At my age, I should have tried again immediately, but with Josh in the picture, I don't know if I want to complicate our lives any further. Daniel's been a fabulous father to Zoe, and I feel guilty I can't reciprocate with his biological child, but I just can't."

"There's no reason to feel guilty," Andrea said. "Daniel knew from day one that you and Zoe came as a package, and he chose to make a life with both of you. Josh came into your lives like a bolt out of the blue and you can't expect to forge a bond in a week. Just do the best you can, and give Daniel enough time and space to work out his relationship with his son."

Hannah took a large gulp of her remaining tea and put the empty cup down. "I know you're right. It's just hard to be patient. I guess it's time for me to collect the kids and head home. Thanks again for being such a great friend."

Daniel was drinking a mug of coffee in the kitchen when the three of them arrived. He stood up and drew his whole family into a brief hug.

Then he turned to Josh. "I'm sorry I messed up your last day here. Unfortunately, my partner was in danger and I had no choice."

"I heard that you rescued her. That was really cool. Can you tell us how you did it?" Josh asked.

"I managed to figure out who took her and headed to his house, but I didn't rescue Brenda. She's tough and smart, and she rescued herself. We found her a few blocks away from the house and took her to the hospital for an evaluation. The bad guys knocked her out, and head injuries can be dangerous."

"Mommy said she's okay," Zoe piped in.

"She is. Thank goodness. I can't imagine doing my detective work without her. Josh, I'm going to make it up to you," Daniel said. He was hoping he could.

"How about I make us a nice family dinner, and we try to enjoy the rest of the evening? How does lasagna sound?" Hannah asked.

"That sounds great," Josh said. "I should probably go pack up my stuff for tomorrow."

"I can help," Zoe offered.

The two of them left the room. Daniel heard a peel of Zoe's laughter as they headed down the hall.

"I was thinking," Daniel said, "about going to Washington sometime over the summer and taking Josh camping in the Cascades. What do you think?"

"Are you talking about a father-son bonding trip or a family vacation?" Hannah asked.

"If I was planning a family vacation, I'd pick a place with room service. Maybe I should have started with trying to get to know Josh better myself before bringing him into our family. I know this hasn't been an easy week for you, and I imagine it was uncomfortable for him as well. I was hoping we could start over."

Daniel knew Hannah had been trying hard all week to relate to Josh, but he could read her well enough to tell when she wasn't happy.

"I'm sorry, Daniel. This might have been easier for me if it weren't for the miscarriage. I would already have tried implanting another embryo, but I'm not sure we can handle Josh and a new baby." Tears were forming in her green eyes, trembling on the lids. Hannah brushed them aside before they wet her cheeks.

Daniel put his arms around her, smelling the citrus

scent of her shampoo. "Why don't we give it a little more time and see what part Josh might really play in our lives. Then we can decide if we want to try again."

She looked up at him. "Not too much time. Remember, I'm no spring chicken and I'm not getting any younger while we wait."

CHAPTER THIRTY-NINE

Josh's flight for Seattle left at 9:00 a.m. so Daniel planned to leave for the airport at 6:30 a.m. Hannah and Zoe, in their pajamas, said goodbye.

Sunday morning traffic was minimal, and Daniel was able to park, escort Josh inside, obtain a gate pass, and get through security in time for them to have breakfast together before the flight.

"I hope you had a good visit," Daniel said.

Josh shrugged. "You know, Hannah could've left Zoe and me alone in the house yesterday. I don't need a babysitter. My Mom trusts me."

"I'm sure she does, Josh, but your Mom knows you. Hannah's just met you, and trust has to be earned."

"Did I blow it with the weed?"

"It didn't help. It's going to take time for all of us, but I hope this was at least a good start. I'll come to Washington this summer and we can work on getting to know each other better."

"Okay."

They heard the boarding announcement as Daniel paid the check, and they walked together to the gate.

Daniel gave Josh a brief hug. He still wasn't sure how much physical affection would be okay.

"Bye, Dad. Is it okay if I call you Dad?"

"Totally okay. Text me when you land in Bellingham so I know you got there safely. See you in the summer."

Daniel watched as Josh, pack on his back, disappeared down the bridge to the plane. He hoped it had been a good start.

From the airport, Daniel drove straight to Hollywood Presbyterian. When he'd phoned the hospital yesterday, Henderson was still in surgery. Since no one had called him to say Henderson was dead, Daniel assumed he'd be awake by now, although he'd probably be too drugged to question.

Parking was easy Sunday morning, and although visiting hours didn't begin until later, his police credentials got him past the security desk. Henderson was in the surgical ICU.

When Daniel arrived, Alberto was seated on a chair, outside Henderson's room. Glancing in, Daniel noted he was still on a respirator.

"Hey, Alberto. Didn't know you'd be here. What's the story? Why isn't he awake?"

"I have no idea. We'll have to ask the doctors."

Daniel walked over to the nurses' station and asked the receptionist if she could locate the doctor in charge of Henderson's case. A few minutes later a young woman in a white coat approached him.

"I'm Dr. Chin. How can I help you?"

Daniel held out his hand to shake hers. "I'm Detective

Ross of the LAPD. I was hoping Mr. Henderson would be awake by now, so that we could find out how he was wounded. Is something wrong? Was there a problem with the surgery?"

"I'm glad you're here Detective. The surgery went well. He had damage to his small bowel, so we had to remove the damaged section and repair it. Bowel contents also spilled into his abdominal cavity, which can cause significant infection, so we washed it out thoroughly and put him on triple antibiotics. Unfortunately, in post-op he had a massive stroke on the left side of his brain."

"Will he have permanent damage? Is he going to die from it?"

"The answers to your questions are yes and probably not. The right side of his body is completely paralyzed, and his speech center is gone. He won't be able to talk and will probably be confined to a wheelchair. We don't have any family contacts for him, so we don't know what his wishes might be in this situation. Can you get me that information?"

Maybe there was a God after all. This was a worse punishment than twenty years in prison.

"Of course, Doctor. I'll call the station and have them pull his records from Human Resources. Thank you for telling me. I'll let the chief know."

He would also let Brenda know she hadn't killed him.

CHAPTER FORTY

IS HEAVY BODY WAS CRUSHING HER ON THE mattress. She could smell his sweat and musk mingled with the blood she had shed. He was holding her wrists above her head with one hand and forcing his knee between her legs. He was so heavy she couldn't move or breathe. His other hand was fumbling with the belt on her jeans. She tried to scream.

"Scream all you like, bitch. No one will hear you."

His weight constricted her lungs. The only part of her body she could move was her head. She watched for his nose to be close enough and tried to hit it with her forehead. She missed. He put a hand on her neck and squeezed.

"Brenda, wake up."

Someone was shaking her. Her brain rose from the depths, and she opened her eyes, squinting at the light.

"Honey, you were screaming and thrashing. You must have had a hell of a nightmare."

"Marcy?" Brenda started sobbing, and Marcy held her. "He was on top of me. I couldn't breathe, or scream, or move."

"No, he wasn't. You defended yourself. You stabbed him and escaped. You're home and okay."

Brenda took a deep breath. "Thanks for waking me. I think what I need now is a long hot shower."

"Followed by breakfast," Marcy said. "When you get out, I'll be in the kitchen"

~

Once Brenda completed her shower, she dressed in her usual work clothes. Her face in the mirror looked wasted, but her hair was clean, and the stitches were not visible. The smell of coffee drew her to the kitchen.

"What are you doing dressed?" Marcy asked. "You were discharged less than twenty-four hours ago. Today should be a pajama day."

"Don't worry. I know I'm on medical leave. When Daniel called yesterday, he said the chief wanted to see me whenever I felt well enough to come in."

Marcy rolled her eyes. "You aren't going anywhere without coffee and breakfast. Furthermore, I'm driving you."

"Yes, Mom," Brenda said, sitting down.

Marcy placed a mug of coffee in front of her, followed by a plate of bacon and scrambled eggs. Brenda dug in. She hadn't eaten anything but some soup yesterday, and she was famished.

"I'm relieved that bastard Henderson is still alive. Too bad I won't get to do the interrogation myself."

"I don't think you're allowed to be both the victim and the cop," Marcy said.

After breakfast, Marcy drove her to the station. "How long do you think your chat with the boss will take?"

"You don't have to wait for me. I'm sure I can get one of

the guys to drive me home, and if not, I'll call a taxi. I promise, once I'm home, I'll spend the whole day sitting on the couch, binge watching NCIS."

"That's too much like work," Marcy countered. "Try Downton Abbey."

~

When Brenda entered the Detectives room, she was greeted with a hug from Daniel and a few cheers from her colleagues.

"You scared the shit out of us, Jordan. We were combing the city for you all day."

"Thanks, guys. I appreciate the effort. It was a bad day," Brenda said.

"The chief wants a chat," Daniel said.

"That's why I'm here."

Brenda walked down the hall to the chief's office and knocked on the door.

Chief Tucker opened it and motioned her inside. "I wasn't expecting you to come in so soon, Detective. How are you feeling?"

"Better, sir. My headache has subsided to a dull throb. I figured you'd want to debrief me as soon as possible."

"It's complicated, Jordan. I've never had a case in which one officer is accused of kidnapping, and another of stabbing a fellow officer. It's going to require an Internal Affairs Investigation, and I'm going to have to put you on administrative leave while that happens. You'll tell your side of the story to your representative."

"Are you telling me that Henderson is going to file a complaint against me for attacking him?"

"I don't think he'll be filing anything, Detective Jordan. Did Daniel Ross update you on his condition?"

"He told me Henderson got through the surgery, so fortunately, I didn't kill him."

"He didn't mention the stroke?"

Brenda's eyes widened. "What stroke?"

"It happened after the surgery. Henderson is paralyzed on the right side of his body and the speech center of his brain is destroyed. As I said, this is going to be complicated. I've asked Detective Ross to take over this investigation."

"I don't get this, chief. Henderson knocked me out, gave me a brain bleed, kidnapped me, threatened to rape and kill me, and when he came for me, I defended myself. I didn't kill him and his stroke is not my fault. The forensics will back me up. Why would Internal Affairs be investigating me?"

"I'm on your side, Jordan, but we have to respect the process. In the meantime, you need to turn in your gun and badge."

"Yes, sir." No point arguing with the chief. This came from above his pay grade. She placed her equipment on the desk.

"One other thing," Tucker said. "You will need to see the department therapist. You've been through a major trauma. You don't get to come back to work until the investigation is over and the doctor clears you."

Brenda nodded and left the office. Hopefully, Daniel could drive her home and she could bring him up to date.

Brenda heard the door open and Marcy entered, leaving her purse and keys on the entry hall table.

"Are you enjoying Downton Abbey?" she asked.

Brenda reached for the remote and turned off the TV. "I keep thinking that if Lady Mary had only been a lesbian, she wouldn't have had to put up with all those boring men wanting to marry her for her money."

"If Lady Mary were one of us, she'd have been permanently in the closet," Marcy said. "Be grateful we weren't born in Edwardian times. How was your talk with the chief?"

Brenda shrugged. "I'm on administrative leave, as expected, and have to see the LAPD shrink before I'm allowed back to work. Internal Affairs is investigating."

"What's to investigate? Is that bastard claiming you went home with him to get laid and changed your mind and stabbed him?"

"Hardly. Apparently, he had a massive stroke after surgery."

"Wow. There really is a God, and she was pissed."

"It's not funny, Marcy. Internal Affairs may decide it was my fault."

"The hell it is," Marcy said. She sat down and reached for Brenda's hands. "You should be proud of yourself. The guy wanted to rape and kill you, and you escaped. The fact that he had a stroke isn't on you."

"He wouldn't have stroked if he hadn't needed surgery."

"You don't know that, and personally, I much prefer his having a stroke to you being dead."

"Me too."

"How about I order take out from the restaurant of your choice?" Marcy suggested.

"Sounds good."

"How long do you think this administrative leave is going to last?"

"Could be months. It depends on Internal Affairs. I have no idea of how I'm going to spend my time while I'm waiting."

"I have a suggestion," Marcy said. "I'm almost done with a major project at work. Why don't we take advantage of this time off, plan our wedding, and go on a fabulous, long, relaxing honeymoon. We deserve it."

Brenda smiled for the first time in days. "That is a great idea, but how about we do the honeymoon first. I'm going to need to wind down before I deal with IA and the shrink. I want to get out of here, someplace where I don't have to think about murder. When we get home, I'll make dinner for my parents and invite them to our wedding."

CHAPTER FORTY-ONE

D ANIEL WAS AT HIS DESK WHEN THE CALL CAME IN from the forensics lab.

"You are going to be one happy detective," the tech said. "The car and the house were a goldmine. You should be able to make your arrests and move on to the next case."

Daniel downloaded the results from the computer. Traces of Brenda's blood and hair had been found in the trunk of McCalls's car, as well as on the mattress in the basement of Henderson's house. There were also blood traces that matched Kevin Chase, and fingerprints of several male prostitutes, including the dead Eddie.

Daniel finished writing his report and gave it to the chief.

"The evidence totally confirms Brenda's account of her abduction, and her theory of the Kevin Chase murder, sir."

"I agree. I'm going to send this to Internal Affairs with my recommendation that Detective Jordan be reinstated as soon as she is cleared by the psychiatrist. You can tell her the forensic results."

"I'll tell her when she gets back from Bali. She thought

this process was going to take long enough for her to have a real vacation."

"I'm jealous. Can't remember my last vacation," Chief Tucker said. "Remind her to make an appointment with the shrink as soon as she gets back. You two are my best team."

"Thank you, sir. I will."

"One more thing. We didn't have enough evidence to hold Donald McCall last week. All I could do was suspend him pending another Internal Affairs investigation. But thanks to forensics, now we do. Take someone with you and go arrest the son of a bitch."

McCall lived in the Valley on Balboa Boulevard. The apartment house dated back to the seventies, and its two stories surrounded a kidney-shaped pool. No one was seated on the faded turquoise plastic chaise lounges that surrounded it.

Daniel and Alberto climbed the stairs to the walkway on the second story. McCall's apartment was a corner unit. The window shades were down and the curtains drawn.

Daniel rang the bell, and nodded at Alberto.

"Hey Don, you home? It's Alberto."

A few minutes passed with no answer, and Daniel rang again.

"Think he did a runner?" Alberto asked.

"Possible. I got a search warrant for his apartment in case we need to break in. He could just be ignoring us."

Daniel reached into his pocket, pulled out a set of lock picks, and set to work. It took less than five minutes to unlock the door.

"Police," he yelled as he pulled his gun, turned the knob

and entered the living room. Alberto followed. They were greeted with silence.

The living room floor was covered in dirty gold shag carpet, the ceiling in popcorn asbestos. The furniture consisted of a large TV and a worn leather reclining chair. A small Formica dining table with plastic upholstered kitchen chairs occupied a breakfast area at the end of the small galley kitchen. A dirty frying pan and breakfast dishes sat in the sink, and the vintage gold refrigerator was empty except for a six pack of Budweiser.

The double bed in the bedroom was unmade, and the small bathroom showed signs of a recent shower and shave. The dresser drawers were filled with underwear and T-shirts, the closet with jeans, slacks, casual jackets and two police uniforms.

"Doesn't look as if he went anywhere," Alberto commented. "There are two empty suitcases in the closet, and all his toiletries are still here."

"Maybe he just went for a walk."

Daniel went over to the corner of the bedroom, where there was a small desk with a computer and a pile of unopened mail. He flipped through the envelopes, mostly bills. In the top drawer he found clipped articles about the Aryan Nation, the Proud Boys and several other white supremacist organizations. The computer, unfortunately, was password protected.

Alberto checked out the bedside table. "Familiar sexual preferences," he said, holding up a pair of cuffs, a belt, a gag and some rope.

Daniel shrugged. "Why am I not surprised?"

"What now?" Alberto asked.

"Let's lock the door from the inside and wait awhile. If he's just out for a walk, he should be back soon. If not, we can see if the building has any security cameras, and we can bring the computer to Izzy."

"What the fuck?" McCall entered the apartment carrying two grocery bags, to be greeted by Daniel and Alberto in his living room, both armed.

"You're under arrest, McCall," Daniel said. "The charge is accessory to murder and kidnapping. I'm telling you your rights."

McCall dropped both bags on the floor. Milk spilled. Oranges and apples rolled. He turned and ran out the door. Alberto followed and brought him down with a tackle.

Daniel watched and grinned. So nice to have a muscular cop, half his age, doing the dirty work. He was a little rusty at football tackles.

"I have the right to my lawyer," McCall said. "You fuckers had nothing on me the last time you questioned me, and you can't accuse me of crimes committed by my partner."

"You can call your lawyer from the station," Daniel said, putting cuffs on McCall and reading him his Miranda rights. "This time we have enough evidence to arraign you. Let's go."

CHAPTER FORTY-TWO

BRENDA SEATED HERSELF IN A COMFORTABLE WING chair in the office of Dr. Lena Schneider, departmental psychiatrist. Dr. Schneider sat opposite her, behind a large walnut desk. This was the last hurdle to getting back to work, and nothing about the doctor was reassuring.

She was in her sixties, with a wrinkled face and ice blue eyes. A pair of metal-rimmed glasses perched on her hawk-like nose, and her silver hair was drawn back into a tight twist. She smiled at Brenda, revealing a mouth of yellowed teeth.

The smile struck Brenda as predatory rather than friendly. This wasn't a woman she wanted to confide in. Brenda planned to keep her revelations strictly confined to her most recent experience. She was thankful the chief had notified her that the Internal Affairs investigation had been suspended, due to the clear nature of the forensic evidence. All she had to do was to prove she didn't have PTSD, and she could return to work. Hopefully, she could accomplish this in a minimum number of sessions.

"You look very tan and relaxed, Detective. Were you on vacation?" the doctor asked.

Brenda had dressed all in white; white linen slacks, a white T-shirt and white sandals. Her tan was smooth and even, her cheeks rosy, and her naturally blonde hair even lighter thanks to the tropical Balinese sun.

"I was. As I'm sure you were informed, I had a life threatening experience a few weeks ago. I thought a vacation might help me to wind down and reenergize."

"And did it?"

"Definitely. During my first week at home, I had nightmares every night and had trouble falling asleep, but once I got to Bali they subsided. I feel ready to go back to work."

"When that happens will be my decision, based on my evaluation. I was given your file, but I'd like you to tell me what happened in your own words."

Brenda took a breath. She'd rehearsed her story at home, planning to present the facts as succinctly as possible.

"I was trying to solve a hate crime. My investigation led me to two new officers at the West LA station. I'd gone there late Friday night to check something on my computer, and as I returned to my car I was assaulted and knocked unconscious."

"Did you see your assailant?" Dr. Schneider asked.

Brenda shook her head. "When I awoke I was in a dark basement on a mattress. My head was bleeding from a cut in my scalp. Luckily, I hadn't been searched and I still had my phone. I used the flashlight app to assess my surroundings."

"I understand you stabbed your assailant. Where did you get the knife?"

"It was hidden in my boot. I had gone on an undercover

assignment earlier that evening and couldn't take my gun. I wasn't expecting trouble, but I took a knife just in case."

Schneider nodded. "How did you come to stab your kidnapper?"

"He came down into the basement, pulled a gun, announced he was planning to rape and then kill me. I had no choice. When he lunged for me I stuck the knife into his belly and ran."

"Very enterprising of you, Detective, but you haven't given me a clue as to how you felt about being kidnapped, or stabbing a fellow officer, or finding out that he will spend the rest of his life paralyzed and mute. When people ignore their feelings and pretend they are just fine after a trauma of that magnitude, it can interfere significantly with their future performance." Small drops of spittle dripped down her chin as she talked.

"For our next session, I'd like you to give some serious thought to your feelings. Until you've worked through them, I won't be able to approve you for duty."

Brenda got up and worked hard at maintaining a calm expression. She had to remember that this woman wasn't on her side. The doctor's job was to make sure her patients were fit to work, and her first loyalty was to the LAPD.

"I understand. I'll make an appointment on my way out with your receptionist. See you next week."

Brenda waited for the elevator, fuming. Her performance hadn't been appreciated by that bitch who controlled her work life. The elevator doors opened to reveal a large number of cops. She entered and pressed the button for lobby, leaning against the doors so she faced them. Her stomach was churning. She used to trust her colleagues with her back, but now, she had to keep an eye on them, be ready to react at a moment's notice.

Two cops got off at the next floor and one brushed her shoulder as he exited. Brenda jerked.

"Sorry," he said, with a puzzled look, as he exited.

She took a deep breath. The parking lot for the building was in the basement, so she'd parked on the street, circling several times until she found a space. Walking quickly with occasional glances over her shoulder, she reached the safety of her car, locked the doors and started the engine.

As she slid into the driver's seat of her car, it occurred to Brenda that it might be a good idea to ask Hannah's psychiatrist friend Andrea to refer her to someone she could trust for some real therapy. The kidnapping wasn't the only issue she had to deal with, and after she came out to her parents at dinner next weekend, she was sure she'd have plenty of material.

CHAPTER FORTY-THREE

"WHAT ARE YOU GOING TO COOK FOR YOUR parents?" Marcy asked.

"Nothing foodie. My folks like old-fashioned American cuisine. I thought I'd just do a Caesar salad, some burgers, and baked potatoes with sour cream and chives. Chocolate ice cream for dessert."

"No kale or quinoa?"

"Definitely not. I want them full and on a sugar high when I break the news," Brenda said. She wasn't sure a good meal would make any difference, but it couldn't hurt.

"Are you sure you don't want me to stay?"

"Trust me, you don't want to be there. This is something I have to do on my own. If I'm tough enough to fight my way out of an attempted killing, I should be able to finally tell my parents I'm a lesbian."

Marcy walked over and gave Brenda a long hug. "Just remember, I love you and am totally on your team. How about I set the table for you and take off? I'll find a good movie. Text me when they leave so I don't come home too early."

Cooking was not Brenda's forte, but the meal was perfect. There was just enough garlic in the salad dressing. The burgers were medium rare, and the twice-baked potatoes hot and fluffy. Brenda steered the dinner conversation to an edited version of her abduction experience, and the reasons for her administrative leave.

"I'm proud of you," her father said. "I always expected you to be a smart cop, but who knew you could be so tough?"

"I didn't," Brenda said, "but you find out what you're capable of when your life is threatened. The chief tells me that LAPD is launching a full investigation of possible infiltration by white supremacist militia groups. I hope you're checking out your staff as well. You need to take this seriously, Dad. We've identified some high ranking officers with questionable affiliations."

"I am taking it seriously. We haven't had many hate crimes lately, but I've asked for some data to see if any of my cops are targeting minorities for arrests. When do you go back to work?"

"As soon as the shrink clears me. Hopefully, that will be soon. She's difficult. Old enough to have trained with Freud. Anyone want chocolate chip ice cream for dessert?"

"Just a little for me, dear," her mother said.

"Two scoops for me," said her dad.

Brenda cleared the table and dished out the ice cream. Dinner had looked good. It was too bad her stomach had been invaded by butterflies, and everything tasted like cardboard.

It was time. She put the plates in front of her parents and sat down. "I have some other news I want to share with you. I'm engaged and planning to get married later this year."

Faith put down her spoon and her face broke into a huge smile. "That's wonderful. We didn't even know you were dating. Who is he? We can have the ceremony in our church. The pastor will be so pleased."

"I don't think so, Mom. I'm marrying my longtime partner and roommate, Marcy. Our church doesn't marry same sex couples."

Faith's jaw dropped and she looked at her husband to gauge his reaction.

James was in the process of swallowing a huge spoonful of ice cream. He slammed his spoon down on the table. Brenda winced.

"How could you do this to us? I thought we raised you right."

Brenda took a breath. "Both of you thought Marcy was a terrific person when you didn't know she and I were partners. I'm planning to spend the rest of my life with her. You can accept the two of us as part of your family, or not. It's your choice, but I'm tired of hiding and pretending to be someone I'm not."

"But you're committing a sin. You'll wind up in hell." Tears were flowing down her mother's face. "Did I do something wrong to make you a lesbian?"

"You didn't do anything, Mom. I was born a lesbian. It's not a choice."

"I'm going to pray for you," Faith said, wiping her eyes with a napkin. "It breaks my heart to know that when I die, I'll never see you again. You won't go to heaven."

James pushed his remaining ice cream away. "I think your mother and I should go home and think on this. I'm sure your brothers will have something to say to you about it."

"What are we going to tell our friends and relatives?" Faith asked.

"Whatever you want," said Brenda. "This isn't about the two of you. It's about me. Marcy and I hope you'll come to our wedding, but if you won't, we understand."

Leaving dessert on the table, James rose, helped Faith up, and guided her out the door.

Brenda sat down and let the tears flow. Finally, she wiped her eyes on her sleeve. She knew her parents loved her, and she'd nurtured a secret hope that they would accept this. Clearly they hadn't, but part of her felt a huge sense of relief to have finally told the truth.

She reached for a spoon and finished the remains of the ice cream carton. Then she texted Marcy: *Come home. Deed is done. The ball is in their court.*

CHAPTER FORTY-FOUR

"WELCOME BACK. I MISSED YOU." DANIEL STOOD up from his chair and gave Brenda a hug.

"I missed you too. I'm glad to finally be back at work." Brenda sat down at her pristine desk, and put her purse away in the bottom drawer.

"It took long enough. Dr. Schneider has a reputation for giving cops a hard time."

"She has a hard job, Daniel. She works for the LAPD. That makes it challenging to put her patient's needs or privacy first. I certainly didn't want to share anything about my personal life with her, although she did probe. I kept it strictly to my abduction and escape."

Daniel's eyebrows rose. "How did you manage that?"

Brenda grinned. "Let's just say, I deserve a membership in the Screen Actors Guild."

"Seriously, Brenda, I'm your partner. Are you okay to come back? I'm talking emotionally, not physically."

Brenda swung around on her chair so she was facing him. If anyone deserved to know the truth, it was Daniel.

"One minute, I think I'm fine. The next minute, my

stomach is in knots. If this experience taught me anything, it taught me that I can take care of myself and protect the people I love. My father always thought I was too much of a softie to be a good cop, but even he was proud of me. I hate the fact that I injured another officer, but I know it was the right thing to do. Horrible as this experience was, it's made me stronger. I'm also in therapy with a real shrink. Someone whose job is to help me handle what happened. I couldn't trust Schneider to do that."

"You were always a good cop, Brenda. I've never doubted your judgment, or feared that you wouldn't have my back in a dangerous situation. Promise you'll tell me if you need support. I'll always have your back."

She leaned over and squeezed his hand. "That's why I'm so glad we're a team. To be honest, Daniel, this experience has made me less trusting of my fellow officers. I know I can count on you and a few others, but everyone else is going to have to earn my trust. Now, are you going to tell me what's happened with my case?"

"McCall caved when presented with the evidence in his car. He admitted that he and Henderson had been picking up prostitutes, and torturing them in their private dungeon. He blamed Henderson for fatally injuring Kevin, but admitted to helping him dump the body at the homeless camp. He also said that Henderson had talked him into helping to kidnap you, and was the one who assaulted you.

"Unfortunately, since Chuck Henderson can't testify or be questioned, it's hard to know if McCall is telling the truth. The prosecution let him plead guilty as an accessory to murder and he'll spend a few years in jail."

"What about Henderson?"

"The prosecutor decided there was no point in prosecuting him. He's mute and paralyzed. The hospital discharged him to a skilled nursing facility in Orange County, near his parents. Unless he has a miraculous recovery, he'll spend the rest of his life there."

"I can't argue with that. I'd rather go to prison, than be in a skilled nursing facility. Those places are awful."

"So, you ready for our next case? We're on call tomorrow."

"You bet. I have one more thing to ask you, though."

Brenda opened the drawer, retrieved her purse and pulled out a framed photo of herself and Marcy on the beach in Bali. She placed it on her desk, and then handed Daniel a cream colored envelope with his and Hannah's names in calligraphy.

"Marcy and I spent some time looking for a wedding venue. We found a great house on Airbnb, up on Mulholland. It's got a big deck with a fabulous view. We've set a date six weeks from now, and the rest of the invitations are going out tomorrow. Here's yours."

Daniel's smile lit up the room. "I'm so happy for you. Marcy is great. What did you want to ask me?"

"We need someone to marry us, and no one knows us better than you do. Would you mind getting ordained online as a Universal Life Minister?"

"I'd be honored."

"One more thing. Do you think Zoe would like to be flower girl?"

"Are you kidding? It'll be the highlight of her year."

Daniel got up and gave Brenda another hug.

"Hey, what's all the excitement about?" Izzy said, walking out of his office.

"I'm getting married," Brenda announced, loudly enough to be heard by the entire room of detectives in their cubicles.

Several of them came over and gave her a high five.

"Who's the lucky guy?" a voice asked.

"Marcy, my roommate," Brenda announced, taking in the expressions of those around her.

There were some smiles and a few shouts of "Congratulations!"

"You mean, you're a dyke," said a voice from the corner of the room. Brenda couldn't see the speaker, but she recognized the voice. It belonged to an older detective she'd never liked.

She turned in his direction. "You bet I am, and proud of it," she said.

"Don't let me ever hear that word again in my station." Chief Tucker said. He was standing at his office door. "I don't tolerate anyone harassing my officers."

The chief walked over and held out his hand. "I wish you a happy marriage," he said.

CHAPTER FORTY-FIVE

Brenda was sitting at her computer in the den when Marcy came in with a bag of groceries and the Saturday mail.

"We've got a bunch of RSVPs," she said, putting the small cream colored envelopes on Brenda's desk.

Brenda opened the Excel spreadsheet she had created to keep track of who was coming. The first group of responses had come from their mutual friends at the LGBT Center and had been overwhelmingly positive and congratulatory. Most of Marcy's favorite colleagues from work had accepted. This pile was from Brenda's colleagues with a smattering of family invitations. Brenda slit them all open and put them in a pile before reading them. She was holding her breath.

Marcy leaned over Brenda and put a comforting hand on her shoulder.

"So, what's the score?"

Brenda had only invited a few of her work mates, including the chief to thank him for his support. "Not bad. The chief is coming with his wife, and Izzy will be there."

She glanced at the remaining RSVPs. "Surprise. My

favorite aunt and uncle are coming. Of course, neither one of them is Evangelical."

"Any word from your parents or brothers?"

Brenda shook her head. "At least your parents are coming. I know you weren't sure they would."

"They've had a long time to get used to the idea of same sex weddings. Your folks are probably still in shock."

Brenda entered a few RSVPs into the spreadsheet and turned. "I regret not having had the nerve to tell them sooner."

"You told them when you were ready. I thought coming out at work would be harder for you. Were you surprised that the chief was so supportive?"

"Stunned and appreciative. He's a good guy, and he's probably experienced his share of bigotry at LAPD during his years of climbing the ladder, so he knows what it feels like."

She turned back to her spreadsheet and finished the entries. "We have 40 coming, 4 regrets and 6 outstanding, all my family. We can probably start doing the seating plan."

"How about lunch first," Marcy suggested. "I got sushi."

As Brenda headed into the kitchen in Marcy's wake, her cell phone rang.

"Mom?"

"I thought I should reply in person to your invitation," Faith said. "I'm coming. I decided that if we weren't going to be together in heaven, I didn't want to miss your wedding on earth. You're still my daughter, and I do love you."

Tears ran down Brenda's cheeks. "I love you too Mom, and I'm happy you'll be there. What about Dad?"

There was a long silence.

"We argued about it," Faith said, "but I couldn't persuade him to come. He feels angry and betrayed, as if somehow this is his fault. He thinks if he'd been a better father you would have turned out differently."

"You know that isn't true. What about my brothers?"

"They'll call you later today. I asked them to wait until we'd had a chance to talk. Both of them are coming. They think their parents need to get their brains out of the nineteenth century. They told us to watch Modern Family."

Brenda laughed. "Thanks, Mom. You'd better go shopping for a Mother of the Bride dress."

"Your mother is coming?" Marcy asked as Brenda ended the call.

"And my brothers. Not my Dad."

"Give him some time. He may come around and be sorry he missed a great wedding." Marcy gave Brenda a hug. "We can't always have everything we want, all of the time."

"You are everything I want. The remainder is just icing on the cake." Brenda returned the embrace, and the two of them sat down to lunch.

Whenever I begin a novel, I like to accomplish three things. First of all, I create a "who done it," a murder and its solution. Secondly, I follow developments in the lives of my two major characters, Dr. Hannah Kline, and her husband Detective Daniel Ross. In the last two novels, I've taken the time to explore the lives and back stories of two of my ancillary characters, Dr. Andrea Marcus in *Murder is a Nightmare*, and Detective Brenda Jordan in this novel, *Murder is a Hate Crime*. Finally, I like to expose my readers to subjects with which they might not be familiar, for example the hunt for extra solar planets in *Murder in the Goldilocks Zone*, or the myriad ethical issues posed by in vitro fertilization in *Murder in Vitro*.

In this novel, I focused on the LGBTQ community, and particularly on the lives of trans people. My novel is set in 2015, but things have only gotten worse since then. So far, as of November 2021, there have been 47 murders of trans people in the US and 375 worldwide, making this year the most deadly on record for the trans community. The victims are most often women of color.

States with right-wing governors at the helm have introduced or passed scores of anti-trans bills. These include Bathroom Bills, insisting that schoolchildren use the bathroom of the gender they were assigned at birth, rather than the one they have transitioned to. Bills have been introduced denying trans girls the right to play on girls sports teams. Anti-trans legislation has attempted to prevent minors from getting gender-affirming hormone treatment. Although not all of this legislation has passed, and some bills have been blocked at the court level, the message of hatred and bigotry is clear.

This barrage of transphobia is detrimental to the mental health of trans teenagers, who have a high suicide rate, and encourages violence and homicide against the trans community. Trans people are more visible now than they were at the time of this novel, but many cis-gendered people are unaware of the struggles of trans people and the hatred directed against their community.

My readers might wonder why a cis-gendered, heterosexual author would choose this particular topic to write about. The short answer is because so many LGBTQ friends and family members have enriched my life and opened my eyes.

Growing up in New York in the 50's and 60's, being gay was simply not a subject that was talked about. Until I was in high school, I was unaware that gay people even existed. My mother's first cousin lived in Greenwich Village with a male companion. His mother lamented the fact that her son never married. My older cousin, far more sexually sophisticated than I was, finally explained it to me.

In graduate school, I joined the National Organization for Women, and met many lesbian couples. Sometime later, my oldest friend, after three failed marriages to men, came out as a lesbian during her medical residency.

Finally, when he was in his early thirties, my younger brother came out. He proceeded to have a forty year relationship and marriage to a wonderful man who recently passed away. It is to my brother-in-law that I dedicate this book.

Among the younger generation, I have a child and a niece who are part of the LGBTQ community, and have met a number of their trans friends. The bigotry and hatred that I see directed toward LGBTQ people infuriates, saddens and frightens me. I fear for the people I love and want to protect.

I hope my readers will enjoy this mystery, and gain greater understanding and tolerance from its setting.

Paula Bernstein
Los Angeles
December, 2021

ACKNOWLEDGMENTS

As always, I'm so grateful for the guidance and editing skill of Linda Schreyer, my longtime editor and writing teacher.

Christiana Miller, my publisher has been a delight to work with and a great support.

I've gotten terrific feedback from the colleagues in my writing class, Laurie Collister, Sharon Dukett, and Rick Draughon.

My husband Uri Bernstein has always been my first reader and finds the mistakes I miss.

Other friends have been available to answer my questions and help guide this manuscript. Special thanks to Hal Bodner and to Elizabeth Saria.

ABOUT THE AUTHOR

 Paula Bernstein is a New York native, who migrated to LA to attend graduate school in Chemistry. She acquired a PhD, an exceptionally nice husband, and the ability to synthesize creative meals from leftovers. Not long afterwards, she escaped her laboratory and attended medical school.

Like her series heroine, Hannah Kline, Paula spent her professional life practicing Obstetrics and Gynecology. When she developed an irresistible desire for an uninterrupted nights' sleep, she retired from her full time practice, and reinvented herself as a writer of medical mysteries.

Learn more about her at her website: https://www.hannahklinemysteries.com/